THE STREETS BETRAYED ME

By

SHANTAE FAVORS

Boom… was the noise that echoed in the silent nights air as Kiesha pulled the trigger on her mothers' killer. Kiesha jumped out her sleep as she had done so many times after having the same dream every night for years since her mother's killer had never been found. It's the same dream every night, except she's never been able to see the killer's face.

By Shantae Favors

DEDICATION

To my family and friends for their unwavering support and belief in my dreams. To the streets that shaped me, taught me, and ultimately inspired this story. And to all those who have ever felt betrayed by the paths they've walked may you find your way back to hope and strength.

Latresha Sweat (Rene) August 18th, 1978- February 17th, 2022

Sister, I will carry your name with me every step of the way on this beautiful journey that I have started. I love you.

TABLE OF CONTENTS

CHAPTER 1

In Buffalo, New York, a young girl named Kiesha lived with her parents, David and Robyn Kelly, who had been together since their college years. The three lived a wonderful life together. Robyn was a boutique owner, and David owned a neighborhood pool hall, which was his side hustle; his real profession was being a street hustler. Kiesha was eighteen and a senior in high school. She stood at 5ft 8 inches with an hourglass shape.

Kiesha only knew her dad as a hard-working man who, when she was younger, was home every night to tuck her in bed; she had everything a little girl could have asked for. David did an amazing job of hiding what he did in the streets from his daughter; she watched her parents work very hard every day. Robyn was a very successful business owner running her clothing boutique.

She was 5′11 with an almond-shaped face with the sexiest chocolate brown skin. Her body was something that the men dreamed about and the woman envied. Her small waist, curvy hips, and juicy booty were just some of the beautiful qualities that Robyn had.

When Kiesha was growing up, she always had lavish birthday parties and her parents drove some of the finest cars in the neighborhood. All the kids in the neighborhood wanted to be friends with her because she had the best of everything. David was such a wonderful father to her; she loved her parents.

Now, what Kiesha didn't know is that David was one of the biggest and most feared drug dealers in Buffalo; the pool hall was the perfect cover-up for so many years. David was able to clean his money there and conduct all his street business without anyone knowing. Robyn would ask David all the time to get out of the street life, but this is who he was. It wasn't hard for her parents to keep their secret from their daughter; David had the streets terrified of the things he was capable of.

One day, Kiesha asked her mother to tell her the story of how they met." Well, one day, I was walking to my dorm, and he was with a group of guys hanging out, and he tried to talk to me; he was so corny,' she said with laughter. But he kept pursuing me; he would not take no for an answer. Then, one day, I was coming from the library, and it started raining, and he just so happened to be there waiting in his car, and he offered me a ride.

That night, we sat in his car, listening to the rain hit the windows as we talked all night about everything. We told each other some of our darkest secrets, and from that night on, we were inseparable. Your father was a year older than me, even after he graduated, he was there after every class to still pick me up. It wasn't hard to fall in love with your father. "Now don't get me wrong, I did have to bust a couple of bitches upside their heads because of my man," Robyn said as they both laughed." Really, Mom Kiesha said, Pop loves you so much I can't see him looking at anyone else but you. "Really,' Robyn replied with a smirk across her face. It was like we were together every day, and one thing led to another: we had you, got married, and the rest is history.

One night Robyn came home early because she was missing her husband, and she was ready to fuck. All through dinner she was sending David the signals that tonight she was getting freaky, and he was ready to accept her invitation. After dinner, Kiesha went into her room to do her homework while her parents cleaned the kitchen. Robyn took Davids hands and positioned them between her legs; David feeling his wife's pussy juices on his fingers soaking up her panties, made his dick hard as fuck. He gazed into her eyes and kissed her passionately. Standing at the sink, David stood behind Robyn and pulled her panties to the side, and started rubbing on her clit as she bit her lip in ecstasy, trying not to moan loud. As her juices ran down her thighs, she grabbed her husband's fingers and put them to her mouth, and sucked the juices from them.

He knew it was time to retrieve to the bedroom as his dick could not wait to enter her soft wet pussy; as they walked into the bedroom, the soft music of Beyonce's song Speechless was playing in the background. He walks into the bathroom and turns the shower on. She starts to suck his dick passionately as the water is running down her plump ass. He grabs her hair as she slowly rotates her tongue around the shaft of his dick to every beat of the music. Licking the head of his dick as the hot water splashes against his shaft and his balls, David couldn't take it anymore.

He lifts his wife into the air and fucks her against the shower glass door. Cum for daddy, he says with a whisper in her ear as he slides his long dick in and out of her. They fucked for hours to where the water had turned cold. Robyn told David tonight she was getting freaky, and she wasn't done. As she laid her husband on the bed, she took him back into her mouth as he positioned himself to be able to see her ass jump up and down every time she sucked his dick.

Get on Daddy's dick was his command, and so she did. She arched her back so that he could see her clit throbbing as he rubbed it while she rode him…dam, Daddy, that shit feels good as fuck. Now it was time for David to take control; he couldn't let his wife have all the fun. He flipped her over to spread her ass. He entered her with strokes of love over and over again.

Who the fuck do you belong to? Was the question being asked every time he hit her spot… Who the FUCK do you belong to? Faster and faster, harder and harder, the strokes got as David's dick started to grow, as the blood rushed to the head of his penis. Baby, I'm fuckin cumin he said. With those words, Robyn relaxed her back and griped Davids's dick with her pussy walls and pulled that nut right out of her husband. He collapsed right on top of her back, kissed her neck, and said I love you as they both fell asleep. Their sex life was always amazing; she loved her husband, and he loved his wife.

CHAPTER 2

In the middle of the night, Robyn lay in her husband's arms and caressed his face. David was a fine-ass man who stood 6ft 2 inches tall. Brown skin and sexy as hell with a big dick, Robyn was loving on her man. She gets up to go to the bathroom, trying not to wake her husband. They were so in the moment that they left all their clothing on the floor, and as she went to pick up her husband's pants, his cell phone was vibrating.

Thinking nothing of it, she opened the message that said WORK. Robyn dropped the phone when she read the message, "Baby, I can't wait to take our trip together; you make me so happy…I love you". Who the fuck is this Robyn said to herself, and she dialed the number; one ring and a voice said "Hey baby, are you still working late?" "Who in the hell is this; and bitch why are you calling my husband?". CLICK… Hello? Robyn looks at the phone and rushes into the bedroom and she wakes David up with a slap to the face. "WTF is wrong with you?" he screamed. Get the fuck up! Who the fuck is in your phone labeled WORK? yeah, ya

BITCH is wondering if you're still at work. David, you told me this wouldn't happen again. Who is she?"

"Man, I don't know what the fuck you're talking about, yo give me my fuckin phone ". He went to grab his phone, and Robyn threw the phone into the wall. David raised his hand and slapped Robyn across the face. "Who the fuck do you think you are questioning me? One more slap landed across her face. Robyn wiped the blood from her lips as the third slap was getting ready to land on her face; she cried out stop, baby, please stop… I love you, and I'm sorry'.

This turned David on, and he said now look at what you made me do; now come here and suck daddy's dick to make me feel better and she did just that. See, what everyone didn't know is that David had been abusing Robyn for years, but he was all she knew, and so she stayed. After he was done, he told his wife that he was sorry and that it wouldn't happen again, and the women meant nothing to him. He fell asleep, and Robyn lay awake thinking of her escape plan, tired of covering up the bruises. It was time to get away from the love of her life.

Kiesha woke up early the following day and went to her parent's bedroom; Kiesha and her mother had a morning ritual of making breakfast together before school. David met his daughter at the door and told her that her mother wasn't feeling well, so she would have to make breakfast by herself; he didn't want his daughter to see what he had done to her mother time and time again. No questions asked, Kiesha said cool pops. I hope Mom feels better. I'll grab something on the way to school instead and they hugged, and she went on her way.

David returned to the bedroom, where Robyn was brushing her hair in the mirror and trying to doctor up her swollen face. He looked at his wife and said Robyn, I love you so much, but you can't make me angry; a man has needs, and sometimes, a husband has to go somewhere else to get those needs met. "Yes, dear, and again, I'm sorry for not being so understanding'. He told her to take the day off and go shopping on him, and he would be home in time for dinner.

As she heard David pull out of the garage, Robyn looked at her face and cried; she was so pretty, but time and time again, her husband made her face and body a canvas for his anger. "I have to leave, but where would we go?" He'll find us if I try to take Kiesha away; he'll find us for sure and kill me. If I'm going to do this, then it has to be done right. She pulled herself together and headed to the bank. Now, when David and Robyn got together, her parents were already dead, and she never really talked about them that much. She always used her mother's last name before she was married because her parents were never married. As she entered the bank, she took out an ID for Robyn Clemons (her father's last name). She put $250,000 into an account under that name and made Kiesha the sole beneficiary of the account. She also left instructions that if anything happened to her, the bank would reach out to Kiesha and Kiesha only to retrieve the money.

After that, she obliged her husband and went shopping for the day. Quarter to 6 was on the clock. Robyn looked herself over once more before her husband and daughter came into the house. Perfect, bruises covered up. She never wanted her daughter to see what was happening because she knew how much Kiesha loved her father. It was the same routine: family dinner followed by friendly conversation; this was such a routine for Robyn and David that there was no evidence of the night before bedroom brawl.

At mid-dinner, David received a phone call, which led him to have to end family dinner time early. The look he gave Robyn, she knew this was not another woman type of business, but this was street business. "don't wait up; I'll check in soon'. David jumps into his ride, bumping the sounds of Young Dolph's Meech track as he pulls on his pre-rolled blunt. Shortly after, he arrives at a warehouse and takes the underground pathway. Putting the car into park, he gets out and is greeted by two of his fellow soldiers, D Mack and Knock.

"Where is he?" David asked; at that time, one of his long-time partners in crime was brought out from the back of a vehicle's trunk. "Aye, YO! Scar, listen, man, let me talk to you; I didn't do that shit, man. I swear, man, I swear." Pleading for his life was David's, aka Scar's old-time friend

Mel. The name Scar was given to David because back in the day, every nigga that crossed him they were left with some scar on their body. ''Nigga shut the fuck up; you don't think I have concrete evidence that you took my dope nigga?''. Nigga I'm the one putting food on YA table, and you steal from me.''

''Ahhhhh, with no warning, Scar broke Mel's jaw. Blood splattered as Mel's jaw shattered into two places. ''Now I will ask again, where is the rest of my fuckin dope nigga? You were at the stash house to pick up the supply, and your bag was short five bricks. ''But…

''Naw nigga I ain't asking no more'', Scar man, please I… BANG… one hollow shot to the dome before Mel could finish his sentence. D Mack and Knock just looked at each other without saying a word. They knew never to cross Scar because they all were just celebrating the birth of Mel's first born with his new wife, and Scar didn't flinch about putting a bullet in that nigga. ''Clean this nigga up, nigga shitted all over himself said, ''Scar said with laughter. Shit like this made Scar's dick hard. He jumped in his ride and sent a text. ''On my way, need my dick sucked tonight. 10 minutes away. '' Jeezy's My President was playing in the air as he rode to his destination.

Scar pulled up to an apartment building right outside of Buffalo and entered the building. What's good, Ma? I'm only here for short; wifey got your text message last night, so she's trippin' right now. I can't stay long'. ''It's all good, Daddy, said Scar's side piece Mia, who was light-skinned, 5ft 7 inches tall with deep dimples and a phat ass to match. '' I hung up when I heard her voice, but anyways, are you ready for our trip to Miami'? ''Yeah, we're all set, now come on over here and take care of daddy'.

Mia had been fuckin David for about two years, and she wouldn't let her feelings get too deep; she did love him, but she loved the money more, so she played her position. Take that shit to the back of your throat Ma, yeah, just like that, oh shit, FUCK! Show daddy you appreciate him, dam you know what I like… Mmmm, Hmm replied Mia, not being able to respond with words because she was choking herself on David's dick. Mia loved suckin' Davids's dick; she liked getting sloppy with that shit. All you could hear through the lyrics of Jhene 'Aiko's Sativa

was the wetness of her mouth and her lips smacking against the head of his dick. Now she knew David had to leave, but shit, she wasn't letting him leave before she got what she needed. Slipping her hand under her pillow while still massaging his balls and the head of his dick with her lips, she pulled out her vibrator.

Touching her clit with her magic wand, she instantly started to squirt all over herself; watching that shit squirt out made David's dick ready to explode. He started pumping faster, trying to fuck her dimples out of the socket. Mia took the pleasure of fuckin herself with her vibrator and pleasuring his balls with it until he couldn't take it anymore. She held his dick in the back of her.

throat until he was begging her to let go, and she slowly released her grip and brought his cum right along with her as she looked up at him as she swallowed...

As David lay there in absolute bliss, getting his dick sucked, Robyn was at home in the same mode while she was lying in bed thinking about her exit plan.

CHAPTER 3

Several months and several beatings had passed, as Robyn was stacking her paper and preparing in one week to leave her family. She understood that Kiesha would soon be turning 19 shortly after her graduation, and if her daughter didn't want to go with her, then she would have to leave her behind because the beatings had gotten worse after David came back from the surprise trip he took.

Robyn's love for David never ended, but she knew that this cycle had to end because she feared that when her daughter went off to live her own life, the beatings might become more consistent and dangerous. Playing the wonderful wife who was happy all the time was something that Robyn was great at; but that last beating started to take something out of her that even she couldn't control.

David had noticed something happening, and he started to have her followed for the last couple of months. Her I Love You was different; her lovemaking was beginning to be different, and she was moving differently but trying to act the same, and it was throwing David off. He was used to watching her without her noticing, even when they were in college, he would skip class to watch her to see who she was talking to.

With her turning him down all the time, there was one night in particular; it was raining as he sat in his car watching her at the bus stop getting drenched, as he miraculously pulled up to offer her a ride. Robyn never knew that David had always made sure that they would be together; he was her prey and her lover, and she had no clue then and even more so now.

Even though David was out there doing his own thing, he was truly in love with Robyn, and he never wanted her to leave him. She was the one person who could make him so angry because he feared that she would leave him one day. He was becoming uneasy because he was starting to feel the shift in his home which was causing him to make some crazy decisions in the streets, niggas were getting knocked off here and there for dumb ass reasons, and the streets knew who was responsible, but no one dared to talk.

Kiesha was one of the people who was talking about the crazy shit happening in the streets, not knowing that it was due to the hands of her father. David sits in his office as Knock walks in. ''What up, my nigga, you were right. She will try to leave you right after your daughter's graduation. I got the nigga at the bank, of course, with some heavy persuasion to let me see her account, and she has over

$250,000 in it and a passport and ID nigga under a whole other name''.

Pulling on his wax-filled blunt, ''Is that right? So, after all these years, she thinks she's leaving; has this dumb bitch learned nothing?''. ''So, what do you wanna do? It's your call said'. Do? I'm not going to do nothing and keep this information between us''. Knock said ''Bet, alright shit nigga hit me up later as he left the pool hall.

David sat there in a daze, thinking how the love of his life was betraying him, and he grew angrier and angrier. ''We need to talk, come to the town ASAP''.... Delete message. David got ready to head home for the routine family dinner. Robyn is looking at David, and David is looking at Robyn, each of them knowing in their own way that shit was about to change for their family.

The following day, as they were making breakfast and talking about Kiesha's graduation, Robyn told David that she would work late at the boutique since she would be closed for the graduation party.

David replied ''me too, love, but I'll be home before you, and we will start dinner. David looked at Kiesha and said ''nothing for the best for my baby girl. If I could shut the whole city down for you, I would for your graduation.'' ''Pops I'm good, just something simple; nothing to big right Ma?'' With a slight smile, Robyn replied '' you know your father, nothing but the best for us'. David told Robyn he would text her to check up on her later, and he left the house. Just two more nights and she was gone; Robyn started thinking about her exit as she looked at her daughter. It was breaking her heart, but she knew she had to leave, and she hoped that one day her daughter would understand.

"Here's the address, make it fast and get ya ass outta the city, $50,000 upfront, and when it's done, your debt with me will be paid up, and don't Fuck this up; this shit can't come back to me understood?", David said to the unknown person on the phone. Once that conversation was complete, David destroyed that phone, brought out his everyday phone, and returned to conducting his business for the day.

Once he returned home later that night, father and daughter prepared a late-night family dinner. 8:46 PM "hey babe, I know you're working late, but I just wanted to say I love you." David sent the text, no response. 9:00 PM: Dam babe, I know you're busy, but can your husband get some love; no response. 9:15 PM No answer when I called babe, and I called the shop; I'm heading over there. If you get this, hit me up.

David gets ready to put his coat on to go to the shop and two police officers approach their front door. "Pops, what's going on? Asked Kiesha, 'I don't know, baby girl. Mr. Kelly? asked the officer. "Yes, David replied, what's going on? Mr. Kelly, may we come in? No, you can tell me what's going on David said. "I'm sorry to inform Mr. Kelly, there's been a break-in at your wife's shop, and she was attacked, and I'm sorry to say she didn't make it.'' CRASH!!! Kiesha's glass dropped out of her hands. ''NOOOOOOOOOO,' they both screamed as David grabbed his daughter. ''WTF happened? Where is my wife? I need to go to her now. It's ok, baby girl. I got you. Mommy, no, why, mommy, why? Kiesha asked as she cried out a painful tune.

Sir, we can take you and your daughter to the hospital, but we have to warn you that you might not be able to see her until the doctors have prepped her body for you to identify her.'' I can drive my fucking self-David said and let me decide when I want to see my wife's body. David and Kiesha headed to the hospital. David, playing his part as the grieving husband, rushes inside the hospital, where they are met by the homicide detectives. ''What happened, what happened? Please, somebody tell me please, OMG God, my wife, my wife''.

Mr. Kelly, I'm Detective Moore. Tell me why your wife was at the store so late tonight. We notice on the door that the shop typically stays open until 5 PM''.Our daughter is graduating.'' at that moment, David's focus switched as he realized what he had done; he turned and looked at his daughter, standing there looking through the glass at her mother's body covered up. Babygirl come here, come to me daughter, and she did and she wept in her father's arms. ''Officer, my wife and I decided to work late tonight because we would be closed due to our daughter graduating; now, please tell me what happened.

''Sir, it looks like someone broke into the shop and assaulted your wife. There is evidence that she did try to fight back, but she was shot in the chest; it looks like she was trying to dial for help, and her phone was in her hand. Currently, there are no fingerprints or clues, but we will keep looking. ''Find the mutha fuckas responsible, or I will, David warned, knowing all along the hitman was already in the winds.

He returned to consoling his daughter, ''Hush baby girl, I got you'. "Mr. Kelly, we're ready for you; said the medical examiner. 'Pops, don't leave me, stay, ''it's ok, baby girl, I have to do this,' I'll be right back. David looked at his wife's lifeless body. Can I have a moment with my wife? He asked. Once the medical examiner was out of the room, David bent down and said to Robyn ''I told you you would never leave me; I will take care of my baby girl now'. Just as the medical examiner was walking back in, David stood up, wiping fake tears, and said ''Thank you, and looked down at Robyn and said I love you, my dear wife'. '' Again, sorry for your family's loss. We will be in touch the detectives said. David drove home as Kiesha just cried and looked out the window.

He hated what he was doing to his daughter, but Robyn knew the price she would pay if she decided to walk away. With graduation day just two days away, Kiesha had given up on that and her dreams of going to college; she was a shell just walking around. ''She's gone, pops, what am I supposed to do now, what are we going to do?'. Babygirl, we're going to live because that's what she would want us to do. Instead of preparing for the biggest day of her life, Kiesha was preparing for the worst day of her life, her mother's funeral.

CHAPTER 4

Several days later, David sent Robyn off so beautifully her funeral was packed with people that Kiesha knew and some she didn't recognize. Her head was all over the place. She remembered her father talking to this beautiful woman in the corner of the church with the prettiest dimples as she thought to herself, who is this? Durning the repass, she asked her father who the pretty lady was, and he told her she was just one of the pool hall customers coming to give her condolences. David played his part as the grieving husband so well, even putting out a reward for any information on the whereabouts of his wife's killer.

After everyone left the repass Kiesha and David were left with a silence inside of their home. David sat at his desk, used one of his anonymous accounts, and transferred $50,000 into an account. Followed by a message using a secured system saying "money sent, I will be in touch, stay low'. Once the transfer was complete, that account was closed as if it never existed. David checked on Kiesha and heard his daughter crying for her mother. He knew that he wouldn't be able to rush Kiesha, grieving her mother; he understood that she had to get through this as she saw fit. He decided to let her be for now, and he continued to build his empire.

The following day, Kiesha lay in bed, eyes swollen shut from crying, wondering how everything changed overnight for her. She lay there looking at her mother's picture. ''Mommy, I will find out what happened to you if that's the last thing I do; you didn't deserve this; I love you.'. Friends and family were blowing up Kiesha's cell phone and the house phone, trying to check in on her and David, but no response was ever given to any of those calls.

She felt no one understood what she was going through; Robyn, David, and Kiesha lived in their own world, or so Kiesha thought. Graduation day came and went. A couple of months had passed since Robyn's death, and to Kiesha, it felt like she was relieving that horrific day over and over in her head. Every day that she woke up was a constant reminder that her mother was gone.

One morning, Kiesha received a text message from her best friend, Monica." Hey, sis, I'm coming over for a movie night, pizza, popcorn drinks, whatever you need, and I'm not taking no for an answer. I love you. Kiesha loved her friend Monica. They had been friends for over eight years; Kiesha was slightly younger than Monica. Monica, who grew up before her time. She was great at school; she graduated early and even received a job at their local bank. She was Kiesha's ride-or-die for life. Monica was 5'6; she had the sexiest chocolate skin and the juiciest plumped lips. She carried herself with confidence because she knew she was a great catch. She always took great care of herself to maintain her curvaceous body. Once Kiesha read the text message, she knew her friend was serious, especially when she looked at the calendar and realized her birthday was less than twenty-four hours away.

Kiesha climbed herself out of bed because she knew Monica was coming; she couldn't avoid her anymore; she knew her best friend loved her like no other. She went to her favorite playlist and chose songs from Xscape, SWV, and TLC. She started cleaning the house, wondering where her father was; she hadn't seen much of him lately, and she wondered if it was because of their doing.

Once she was done cleaning, she climbed into the shower and let the water wash her tears away. Stepping out of the shower towel wrapped around her, she chose a nice fluffy pajama set and threw her hair in a slick back ponytail. ''Hey pops were, are you? Are you ok was the text message she sent out? Several minutes later, he replied, conducting some business, I'll be home tonight, baby girl. Let me know what you would like to do for your birthday. I love you.

Once David sent the message, he went back to conducting his business; that's right, baby sucks daddy's dick, yeah just like that; daddy likes it when you listen to him. He had started spending more and more time with Mia since Robyn's funeral. Kiesha walked to her parent's room and placed her hand on the doorknob. After a couple of minutes of standing there, she opened it and walked in, realizing this was the first time of her being inside their room since Robyn was gone. "Kiesha looked at Robyn's robe across the bed as she picked it up and smelled it. She thought to herself, wow, it still smells like her. "Mommy, we had so many plans for my birthday, college, and my life in general; I can't do this without you, mommy I need you'. She lay on her mother's side of the bed as a tear fell from her face. I will never be the same again mommy, never.

Around 8 pm, Monica was at Kiesha's door with everything in hand, just like she promised. She was met with hugs and kisses. "Hey, sis, tonight is a little pre-birthday pampering from me to you. We can laugh, cry, yell whatever you want, but tonight is yours, sis, and I'm here with you. Thanks, girl shit, we will probably do them all; it's been rough Bitch roll up," Kiesha said.

Monica brought out a bag and said Bitch already done. I'm not wasting any time. Where's the blender? It's daiquiri time and turn some music on. The two friends danced the night away and told some of their best stories about Robyn. Down five blunts and three daiquiris each, Kiesha started to cry. Monica held her best friend, "let it out, sis; let it out.

As David approached his front door, he could hear the music and the smell of weed. He didn't have a problem with Kiesha smoking, and he understood why she would even more so now. He walked in on Monica, holding Kiesha as she wept in her arms; ''hey, Mr. D, Monica said we're alright over here'. David came closer and said how's my girls and took Kiesha in his arms. ''Baby girl, I'm not rushing you, but you must go out; your birthday is tomorrow. Let's do something, your mother would want that. ''Her gravesite'' Kiesha said. Monica and David looked at Kiesha. I want us to go to her gravesite; we haven't been since the funeral, and I would love to clean it off and put some new flowers pops, can we'? ''Anything for you, Monica, will you come with us? We can all go to lunch afterward. Robyn's gravesite had a beautiful picture of her on the tombstone; David sat in silence as he missed his wife. It wasn't that he didn't love her, but his plan was for her never to leave him, at least not on her own. They sat and talked and said their goodbyes once again to Robyn. Happy Birthday to me said Kiesha; I love you mommy.

CHAPTER 5

Months after the death of Robyn, things were falling back into place for David, but Kiesha was going through the flow of things. Deciding on what to do with her life was her everyday question. She was trying to keep herself together, but every day was a struggle that she kept to herself.

One night Monica talked her into going out to a party, ''Bitch you gotta get out; you've been sitting in this house now for a minute, chick. I know Mrs. Robyn is cussing you and me out, so come on, best friend, get sexy as hell, and let's go. This party is supposed to have Hella niggas there''. After several attempts, Kiesha agreed to go.

Stepping out tonight, Kiesha put on a skin tight, short black dress that showed her curves to perfection. Her hair was up in a bun, the perfect combination that said I'm the shit. She looked gorgeous. She thanked her friend for getting her out of the house.'' Girl, I needed this.'' Yeah, you did, best friend, but you need some dick in ya life too, girl'' they both laughed as they drove off listening to Chris Brown's Under the Influence.

Driving up to the gate, all you could hear was the music banging and the strong smell of the best weed. '' Girl, whose party is this? Kiesha asked her friend. '' Shit, one of my clients from the bank, he said, his best friend is throwing it. He's always inviting me to something, and tonight, I thought this was the best time to take him up on his offer. Bitch, it looks like this nigga got some money; let's just stay for a couple of hours, and then we can bounce Monica said. Yeah, we can wait for a short; I need to dance some steam off Kiesha said

Walking into the house, it was beautiful; there was beautiful artwork and furniture, and the whole décor screamed maturity, Kiesha thought to herself. Monica introduced Kiesha to her client from the bank. His name was Dale, and he introduced them to his best friend. Now, when this man turned around, all Kiesha saw was sexiness. Brown complexion with the sexiest goatee with the beard to match,6ft 7 inches tall, and his dreads were hanging beautifully. Kiesha yelled out ''DAM' 'as she was already having thoughts of pulling his dreads as he ate her pussy. Monica looked her way and laughed because she knew what her best friend was thinking.

The man approached her, reached for her hand, and introduced himself. ''Hello beautiful, my name is Jamal, and you are?'' '' Kiesha,' she replied. ''Thank you for coming, and please save a dance for me, pretty lady. He excused himself to entertain his other guest. Kiesha and Monica looked at each other, and when Dale walked away, they both said "BITCH!!!". Trying to stay calm, she said to Monica "girl, he's fine as hell, he just made my pussy wet. "See, I told you needed some dick bitch, he's fine, but he ain't for me. Enjoy, best friend, Monica said as she grabbed them both a drink.

They started dancing, and Kiesha was a great dancer; she knew how to let her body work itself to the music. Listening to Rihanna's song Love Song, Jamal stood in the background watching Kiesha from afar, already knowing that he was going to make her his. He felt it, and so did his dick. Hours and hours passed as the ladies danced. Finally, Jamal approached Kiesha and grabbed her by the hand to initiate a conversation.

"So, pretty lady, what did I do so right in my life for you to walk into it? Kiesha chuckled and said I don't know, you tell me; better yet, let's ask your wife, where is she?" No, love, I'm single and still looking, but I hope to change that tonight. Anyways, what's a young, pretty girl like yourself out past your curfew? What's your age, beautiful? Nineteen, and I'm all woman she responded, and yours? Oh, I'm twenty-five. Is that a problem, love he asked. Not at all, Kiesha said, hardly being able to focus because her pussy was doing all the thinking for her at that moment.

The conversation was going so well that when Monica was ready to leave, Jamal offered to drop Kiesha off so they could continue talking. Their conversation went on all night; they talked about some of everything, and they didn't let the fact that she was nineteen and he was twenty-five get in the way. They started spending every day together. She never wanted to leave Jamal's side; their endless days became their endless nights and then months.

So, she decided to move in with him the night he asked her to, ''Girl, are you sure you're not rushing into this?'' Monica asked her. '' It feels right, girl, and I love him. It's been a couple of months, and I haven't felt whole since my mom was taken away from me, and he makes me feel complete, shit plus my pops ain't never here anyways; I've been hearing he's been laid up with some chick.''

Ding Dong, Kiesha goes to the door, and a tall man with glasses hands her a big yellow envelope. ''What's that?'' asked Monica. *''Dear Kiesha, I know this may come as a surprise, but I wish I could give you this in person. Babygirl, I love you so much. You are the best thing that I did in my life, and I want you to be happy, and fall in love and raise your own family. Here's a check for $250,000. Please keep it to yourself and make your dreams happen. I love you forever, baby girl, Love Mom'.*

Kiesha sat on her bed with tears falling down her face; she missed her mother so much, and she had so many questions with no answers; the 1st question was, who in the hell was Robyn Clemons? Secondly, why couldn't she tell her father? ''Is this check real?'' asked Monica while holding it to the light. To the bank, we go. ''So, are you going to say anything to your dad? ''No, if my mom told me not to, she must have a good reason.'. Maybe she thought my dad wouldn't let me do whatever I wanted with the money, but we will never know. She didn't know that David already knew about the money, but if he were to let on that he knew about the cash David would have to admit he also knew that she was trying to leave him.

She finished packing and was again preparing for another change in her life, starting a new one with Jamal. As she was walking through the house, in every room she passed, she remembered laughter or stories between her mom, dad, and herself. Damn how things have changed, she thought to herself.

CHAPTER 6

Over the next couple of months, Jamal and Kiesha were adjusting to living together, and before they knew it, a year was approaching, and things were better than ever between them. Kiesha was still mourning her mother, but she was starting to rebuild her life.

"Girl, I'm thinking about going back to school. It's been a year, and things are changing so fast for me; Jamal was talking about babies the other night, which got me thinking about what direction I want my life to go. Ok, chick, let's not get too serious. You're young, and you still have so many things to do in life that you've talked about; take your time" Monica said to her friend. The look Kiesha gave Monica made Monica say" ok, I get it, leave it alone; so anyways, you also have a birthday coming up, and I heard Jamal mention this big ass party he's planning; do you need my help with anything? Monica asked her, Girl, no, my man has everything under control; just show up and show out.

Kiesha reached out to her father to invite him to the birthday party. Things seemed to be moving so fast that she hadn't realized that Jamal and her father hadn't met yet. Of course, he agreed to come; with no more routine family dinner nights, David had completely gone into hustlers' mode; he was living & breathing the drug game. The night of the party, Kiesha said to Jamal, " Babe, it's time for you to meet my father. He's been out of town, and he'll be back tonight for the party. I'm a daddy's girl, and I need his approval." Jamal replied we should have already taken this step; I'm ready.

The best food and drinks anyone could ask for. Jamal didn't give the event planner a limit, just as long as Kiesha was happy. Now David knew about his daughter dating Jamal, but he hadn't heard much about him in the streets except that he was from Memphis. He missed his daughter, and he was eager to see her. Pulling up to Jamal's house, David thought to himself, this nigga got a little paper, let's see what he's about.

"Pops,' Kiesha yelled when she saw her father as she jumped into his arms. "Babygirl, omg, I have missed you; gorgeous as always…a daddy's girl. Kiesha motioned for Jamal to come to where she and her father were for an appropriate introduction. What's up, man, I'm David. "Jamal Black, sir, it's nice to meet you'. I see you are taking great care of my baby girl'. "Shit, what kind of shit you into?" as he laughed it off. (Naww nigga fa real, what kind of shit?") David thought to himself. Jamal shook hands with David as he introduced himself; how are you, sir and I dabble in investments.

"Investment, huh?" David replied. Yeah, I received a settlement and decided to invest my money, and it hasn't steered me wrong yet'. Kiesha looked at Jamal as she realized that was something she didn't know. Then she said to her father, ok, pops, stop interrogating my man; let's go and have some fun.

They partied hard all night, but David didn't stay too long. David thought this dude might be good for my baby girl, but I'm still going to continue to look into him as he was leaving the party. The early morning was approaching. As their guests left the house, Kiesha thanked Jamal with a long, passionate kiss. He lifts her chin to his face and told her he loved her. She looked down as she noticed the bulge coming through his pants.

He lifts her onto the kitchen counter as she puts one leg up on his shoulder; he kisses the inside of her right thigh as he moves up towards her love box. Ohhh, she lets out a moan when he licks her clit and takes it in with his bottom lip. He looks up at her and mouths the words your mine forever as he continues taking her pussy lips into his mouth as his early morning breakfast. Jamal fuck baby, fuck, she says oh my god baby, don't stop. She lays back on the kitchen countertop as he stands up. He opens the fridge to grab the chocolate drizzle.

He looks at Kiesha as the light from the window highlights her erect nipples, as he slowly pours the chocolate over her nipples, down her stomach, and onto her pussy. He starts kissing her all over her neck and then to her nipples while his dick is standing at a full erection, waiting to enter her pussy. Her pussy was throbbing, begging for him to enter. "Not yet, baby, I want to take my time with you tonight" as he takes her nipples back into his mouth and starts to rub on her clit, mixing in the chocolate with her pussy juices. Leave the door open by Bruno Mars played over the kitchen's Bluetooth speaker as she was moving her hips against his fingers. Kiesha was Cuming back-to-back. "Fuck daddy, yes, deeper daddy. He slides his hand to her neck and begins to apply soft pressure; with his left hand, he places his dick inside her as they both let out a long-awaited sigh." Happy birthday baby" he whispers to her as he grips the edge of the kitchen counter and pushes his dick into her, and they fucked for hours that morning.

CHAPTER 7

Kiesha woke up looking for Jamal late that afternoon, and she went downstairs to his office; as she was approaching the office, she could hear him talking to someone and it seemed serious. The door to the office was slightly open, and when Kiesha pushed it a little further, all she could see on Jamal's desk were bricks and bricks of cocaine. Jamal and Dale looked up as Jamal said "Kiesha, what are you doing down here?" Fuck what am I doing down here? What the hell is going on? Where did all these drugs come from, Jamal? You're a fuckin drug dealer nigga?".

Dale looked at Jamal "I'll catch you later, my nigga; handle your business. Kiesha, happy birthday again, the party was the shit". As Jamal was bagging the product back into the black duffle bag, Kiesha grabbed his hand and said " Stop, babe, talk to me; if this is a part of your life, then it's part of our life, and I want in on it. At that moment, Jamal knew he was right about her; she was down for him, and he fell deeper in love with her.

He sat down at his desk and started sharing his story of how his older brother Calvin got him into the street life after he received his settlement when he was seventeen.' 'Babe, my brother Calvin was everything to me, and I always wanted to be just like him; yeah, he was a street nigga, but he was my big bro". "Was? Babe, why do you keep saying he was? Where is he? Jamal replied "Our parents never looked after us, and they always left him to pick up the pieces, but that made him grow up a lot faster; he never had a childhood'. He ran the streets to provide for us. When I was about 15, I was hit by a car, and two years later, I received a significant settlement. Calvin introduced me to the street game because he said as long as I knew how to hustle, I would always be able to feed myself even if he was gone.

A year after following in his footsteps and picking up on everything that Calvin taught me, my brother was shot and killed; man, that shit hurt bad, baby, but he always told me no matter what to keep pushing. I found my own connect and started building my brand. Things were finally looking up, so I decided to make my move to Buffalo, and I have been here ever since. "Baby, why didn't you tell me any of this? as she wiped a tear from his face. Shit, babe, there's just some shit I don't talk about, but I'm glad we are. "Look at you got a nigga shedding tears and shit," as he let out a laugh.

The investments are just a cover-up, but back in Memphis, I was running shit, and like I said shit, I decided to come to

Buffalo to expand. ''Sorry for not being honest with you, love, but you don't need to have any parts in this; ya pops will have my fuckin head if he found out''. ''Let me worry about that; if we're building a life together, I want to know everything to protect each other. She pulled a chair up, ''So teach me, Daddy,' they laughed.

From that moment on, Jamal taught Kiesha everything from pickups & drop-offs, cooking product, weighing them up, and even pricing. Everything she needed to know to be a successful drug dealer. Surprisingly she was good at it; she started handling little shit here and there for Jamal. She was gaining much respect in the streets, but everyone knew not to say anything to her father. Bringing Kiesha into his operation along with Dale, Jamal was moving more weight than he could handle; he had heard of an Ole G named Scar, who was the biggest drug dealer out there, but even with his connects in Buffalo, he could not learn the identity of Scar. Things were going so well that Kiesha started having more control over things. She was good with money, making deals, and finding new connections. She was known for not taking any shit from anyone. Robyn's death turned Kiesha dark on the inside, and all it took was the drug game to bring it out.

CHAPTER 8

David was spending more time out of the States; he was already so well-connected that he only returned if needed. He had his top soldiers in place, and his kingdom was where it needed to be. Lying in bed with Mia, she said ''baby, I want to get married'; we've been doing this for a minute now, and I want more.'

''Don't start that shit as he pushed her off him; I already told yo ass before; marriage is not an option for me. Robyn was the love of my life. Mia looked at him and said, ''But she was the love of your life, and yo ass was cheat… ''SLAP''!!!

''WTF D,'' Mia said as she held her face. ''Listen, you knew what this shit was, Mia; I ain't saying I don't fuck with you, but there will never be; you will never be Robyn. Understood? Yes, she replied, as she laid back down on his chest. David's phone vibrates, letting him know that he has a message coming in. ''No new information on this nigga boss''. He replied' Keep looking; it's something there, I feel it. I'll be back next week.

Now while David was out of town thinking his daughter was this young woman busy falling in love and finding her way through life, Kiesha was making some boss-ass moves. More and more Jamal was becoming impressed with Kiesha's actions. She was young, but she was a fast learner, and she meant business. One night one of their street runners got locked up, and the word on the street was he was thinking about making a deal.

With no money, somehow, the runner found out he made bail. When he left the jail, Kiesha and Jamal were waiting for him at the corner. They had someone bail him out so that no trace could be led back to them. "What's up, fam? Glad to be out," the young man said. " That's what's up nigga. You knew we were coming. We're family, we in this shit together, let's get something to eat nigga". Kiesha told him he could sit in the front with Jamal, eager to escape the jail; the runner didn't ask any questions, so he hopped right into the front seat.

"A nigga hungry Mal, shit where are we going to eat? he asked, noticing they had been driving for a minute. Kiesha was sitting in the back hands sweating because she knew what was coming, what had to be done, what she had to do. Shit, you know Kiesha, she had a taste for some crazy shit, lol; we almost there, Jamal said. As they turned down a street with no traffic, Jamal pulled over and handed the street runner the blunt.

After one pull, he said, dam, a nigga is hungry as hell, he went to turn around to say something to Kiesha, and then BOOM.!! She shot him right in the face. Smoke, flashes, and a painfully loud noise were the three main things Kiesha focused on inside that car, not the fact that she had just blown someone's face right the fuck off. ''Oh, shit babe, you bodied that nigga, you good?'' Babe, you good?? Jamal asked.

Kiesha looked at him with no remorse and said it was us or him. Daddy, I fuckn love you''. Jamal picked up the half-bloody blunt and puffed and puffed and passed it to his lady. My ride or die, he thought to himself. They buried his body and got rid of the car by sending it up in flames and jumped in the ride they had stashed away as their getaway car bumping Beyonce & Jay Z's On the Run, and they went home showed and fucked and showered some more. Kiesha was like her father in more ways than she knew.

Date night was approaching, and Kiesha needed to do some shopping; she called Monica up to meet her at the mall, ''hey girl, can I talk to you for a minute? Monica asked her. Listen, I'm worried about you. I'm not trying to step on his toes, but since you've been with Jamal, it seems like you've changed; I'm just worried about you', Monica said. ''We're good, boo, don't worry, but I will correct you on something; Jamal didn't change me; the mutha fucka who killed my mother changed me.'' Now let's do some major shopping, girl, it's on me' Kiesha said as she hopped out of the car. They spent the entire day shopping. Before they went their separate ways, Monica bent down to look at Kiesha through her passenger window." I love you; chick and I only want the best for you. " Kiesha replied, "I love you too, sis, and trust I got the best. Kiesha continued her drive home in silence.

"Hey, babe, how are you feeling,' Jamal asked Kiesha as he entered the bathroom while she was soaking in the tub. I feel tense, Daddy, as she looked at him with her puppy dog eyes, "Is that right he asked as he started to roll up his sleeves. He turns Chris Browns Back to Sleep song on the speaker as he bends down next to the tub; he says, "The water feels good" as he slides his hands under the water to pleasure the love of his life.

"That's it, baby, let ya man take the stress away" as he finger fucks her under the water, in between Jamal's fingers and the water splashing against her clit. Kiesha was letting out moans back-to-back. Right there, oh shit daddy. 'Tell me you love me" Jamal said as sits up on his knees to kiss her while still underwater fuckin her.' 'I love you, baby, oh shit... "Cum Now!! And with those words from Jamal, Kiesha released herself.

Jamal was the only man who made Kiesha feel the way she did. She loved him so much, but there was a part of her that Monica was right about. Ever since the death of her mother over a year ago, she hasn't been the same. Kiesha was turning into someone she did not recognize. ''Mal, can I talk to you?'' Baby, I want you to help me find out who killed my mother; my father doesn't talk about her anymore, and the police closed the case. It's like her or her killer never existed''. She started to tear up. ''Kiesha baby, you know that I love you, but right now shit is hot. We can't go around knocking niggas off trying to find your mom's killer; it won't be good for business.''.

After we lost our connection two months ago, that nigga Scar has been blocking all our shit,'' and we are just now getting back up top, and nobody knows who this nigga is, so we have to be careful that we don't have any run-ins with this nigga, shit is crazy right now babe.'' ''Give it some time, and I promise I got you', he said as he kissed her and exited the bathroom.

As Jamal left the house, Kiesha called her pops,' What's up baby girl?'' Pops, are you back in town? Can we meet for lunch today? I want to talk to you about something. Yeah, I landed last night. Come by the pool hall; I'll lock it down, so we won't be disturbed.

After all her morning drop-offs and pickups, she went to the pool hall for a much-needed long overdue talk with her father. As she pulled up to her father's place of business, she thought to herself wow, I haven't been here in over a year. Mom, things have changed so much since you've been gone, but I promise to find out who took you away from us and make him pay.

Kiesha greeted her father with the biggest hug ever; just from the hug David knew that this visit wasn't just about her missing him. ''What's going on baby girl, let's talk'. ''Pops, it's been over a year since Mom passed, and it's like everyone is forgetting her: the police, you, everyone. Why did you sell her shop? Why did the police stop looking for her killer? What? Wait, Baby girl, slow down one thing at a time. David felt a little overwhelmed with the questions coming at him. He knew one day they would; he just wasn't prepared for them today.

''I miss your mother every day; she was my everything, and just because you don't hear about it doesn't mean that I'm not trying to find out who took my wife because she was my wife before she was your mother'. There's no information pops. It seems like she never existed; it's so hard to ride past her boutique knowing she's not there, knowing that the entire thing is nonexistent. David hated seeing his daughter hurt, but simultaneously, he felt it was all Robyn's fault. He thought to himself, "See what you did to our daughter; all you had to do was behave, and you would still be here, but you had to be fuckin selfish.

He assured his daughter he would never stop looking for Robyn's killer even though he already knew the exact location of the person, but that would be a secret he vowed to take to the grave. Father and daughter continued their lunch together; this was the first time they sat down together, each holding secrets of their own. David received a call telling him his help was needed to conduct some business, so he ended the lunch with his daughter, "Oh, is Jamal only in investing? He asked Kiesha. "Yes, pops" just investing he's somewhat of a nerd. Why Pops, what's up? 'Nothing, baby girl, just making sure you're good. I'm glad he's making you happy; you deserve that. He does pops and listen I'm not trying to give you a hard time, but I just want Mommy to be able to rest in peace finally, and she can't do that until that muthafucka is found (sorry, pops). She said she never cussed in front of David; she always showed him the utmost respect. They finished their lunch and said their goodbyes.

After Kiesha left the pool hall, David's right hand, Micky, came to discuss the next shipment coming in. "Yo, what up my nigga? This next batch coming through is pure as shit; we are going to need some extra buyers. What time does the shipment land? David asked. Shit, in about forty-five minutes, Mickey said. David sent numerous text messages that said, "Pool game tonight, fellas 8 pm sharp, be prepared to spend no less than $20,000.' Once the text was sent out, everyone who opened it read the message, took the sim card out, and destroyed the phone. This was their system for years. David's product came from overseas; there were only two people who knew who the connect was: David and

Mickey. He kept it like this because, besides Micky, he didn't trust anyone.

Business was booming, and Micky was correct; this dope was in its purest form. David's booming business was causing some hiccups in Jamal's business. The product was running low, and Dale and Jamal ran out of options. Let's take that trip to Miami, bro Jamal said to Dale, I have a connect out there who might have a business opportunity for us because our shit is getting stepped on here, and it's costing us money. Dale agreed, and they set things up to head out of town. Jamal went home to tell Kiesha about his plans.

CHAPTER 9

Walking into the house, Jamal could hear Muni Long's Hrs & Hrs; as he kept walking, there were rose petals and candles leading into the living room. Once he entered the living room, there was a projector screen on the wall; behind it was the silhouette of Kiesha's body slowly dancing. The light from the projector made her body look so sexy to him.

He saw the chair in front of the screen for him to sit in, with a note that said tie one arm to the chair, Daddy and enjoy a glass of champagne. He listened to his woman's commands. She danced behind that screen to the music of Usher, Jazmine Sullivan, and SZA. His dick grew harder and harder, just watching her knowing that he couldn't touch her.

Finally, she made her way to her lover, took a sip of his champagne, and tongue-kissed him as if they were talking to each other. She then tied her hand to his hand and straddled her man as he slid right inside of her. Using his free right hand, Jamal cupped her ass as she bounced and rotated her pussy on his dick while she used her free hand to place her nipple inside of her mouth and continuously sucked on it.

Being able to use just one free hand was ok to them because they both knew each other's body so well. As their fuck session grew more intense, she looked him in his eyes and untied both of their arms, and he picked her up and carried her to the floor, dick still inside of her. They had such a good chemistry with each other. Jamal always made sure Kiesha was sexually, mentally, and emotionally satisfied.

As they lay in each other's arms, Jamal concluded that she would be his wife one day. Ring shopping starts tomorrow, he thought to himself. In the morning, during breakfast, Jamal and Kiesha started talking business. ''Let's run the numbers, babe Kiesha said'', ''shit, the product is running low, and our old connect decided to go into business with someone else, and they cut us out, so I suggested for us to go to Miami this weekend to meet a new connect.''

''Ok, babe, do what you need to do. Do I have enough to make the drop-offs while you're gone?'' ''Yeah, we're straight, and there's a little money in the stash for you to hold you over until I get back; I'm just not understanding what's going on; lately, it just seems like all of our shit is being put up against a roadblock, but I promise I'm going to figure this shit out. ''Now, tonight I want to take you out to dinner, let's get dressed up and party tonight.''

Hell yeah, shit, I need a drink or two tonight, babes; let's do it. ''Yeah, let's call Monica and Dale; we all need a break anyway,' Jamal said. As Jamal left the house Kiesha took a moment to walk through the house that had nothing but silence but spoke with echoes. "Wow, she thought to herself, I love this man, and look at everything that he has given me, everything that he has shown me. Mama, I wish you were here to meet Jamal; he's such a provider, just like Daddy was. I know you would love him, as a tear slid down her face.

Music, drinks, weed, and more weed was everything on the menu; they were out enjoying life together. Kiesha looked at Jamal, Monica, and Dale, her newly formed family. She was grateful for them all. As the night was coming to an end Jamal requested the DJ to stop playing the music and requested champagne at their table. Drinks were held up in the air.

As per request from Jamal, the DJ played On the run by Jay Z and Beyonce (this was their song) " Jamal looked at Kiesha and said "baby, you have changed my life; you are my ride or die as I am yours, I fuckn love you". "Aww baby, I fuckn love you too; this shit is for life". She said in return. I'm glad you said that because I want to spend the rest of my life with you. Will you marry me?" As Jamal spoke those words, he brought a beautiful box to give to Kiesha. Once opened, the box lit up to showcase a 10-carat one-of-a-kind princess-cut diamond engagement ring.

Kiesha and Monica both hollered and said "YES', everyone looked at Monica' 'Oh shit, my bad, go head girl' as everyone laughed. "Yes, baby, yes baby," Kiesha said as she jumped in

Jamal's arms and kissed her man like there was no tomorrow. ''Turn that shit up, DJ,' Jamal said as the newly engaged couple danced together.

They didn't want the night to end. Congratulations, the entire club said in unisex. ''Come here, Daddy let me dance for you; let me ride that dick club style,'' Kiesha said as she clapped and rotated her ass all over her future husband's dick. With every hard beat to the music, it was matched with a hard-ass check clap on Jamal's dick. This was life, and it could only get better for them, Kiesha thought as she looked at her soon-to-be husband.

On the ride home, the air was filled with love as the lovebirds listened to Toni Braxton's, How many ways, and Tamia's Stuck with me (one of her mother's favorite songs). Jamal added it to their play list because he wanted her to have some part of her mother with her that night. ''Baby, you make me so fucking happy, and when you come back from Miami, we are going to do shit so big, I want an engagement party, and I need to pick out dresses; oh, I have to call my father. He's out of town again'. Easy baby, the world is yours, Jamal said, laughing. I promise when I get back home, we will start planning, but let's enjoy tonight'.

They finished their drive home and still sang their favorite R&B love songs. Once home, Kiesha fucked her man, her future husband, to sleep. She lay on top of his chest and fell asleep to his heartbeat. The following day, Jamal was preparing to leave, giving Kiesha a rundown of how business was supposed to go while he was gone for the weekend. She told him to be careful and to watch his back, and she kissed him and sent him on his way.

Jamal met Dale at the airport, and they hopped on a plane to get ready to meet their new connect. The next three days, Kiesha held shit down for them, and Jamal was holding shit down in Miami. They met with the new connect, the prices were a little different, but Jamal and Dale knew they could make anything work. The connect reassured them that if things went well with this run, they would continue to do business together. The two friends conquered what they came to do, and the connection last night showed them the time of their lives.

Kiesha was looking at the progress she had made over the weekend. Everything, just as she suspected, went great; the runners were making their drop-offs at the stash houses left and right; she couldn't wait until her future hubby came home so that she could show him how she ran things, she even had a few ideas she wanted to run by him. She was proud of herself, even if it was just for the weekend, she got a solid taste of what it was like to run shit completely by herself, and she wanted more.

CHAPTER 10

Before heading back to Buffalo, they stopped at Dale's house in Dunkirk to talk before Jamal headed home. The new connect gave Dale and Jamal one week to get rid of his product, and then he would decide if he would work with them. Everything was on the line for them, so they had to make this work. ''Shit, we need to take this shit to the niggas in Ohio; there's more than enough to go around, and we only have one week to get rid of these twenty bricks nigga''.

Be easy, D, Jamal said. We are going to play this shit out right; between you, me, and Kiesha, we can each split the shit up. You can run your shit on the west side, I'll take the east side, and Keisha can take the South Buffalo areas and shorty gotta couple of licks in Niagara Falls. 'Yo, Kiesha is a real one, my nigga; she is holding us down. I thought she was going to flip that day she caught us, but shit, she jumped right in with us, sis is the shit. ''Yeah, you have no idea nigga, Jamal replied, thinking about their recent incident in the car with the street runner. Jamal trusted Dale, but this was a secret that he and Kiesha created a new bond over, and no one would know that secret. To the world, that nigga left and went back to NYC, no questions asked.

Ok, bet nigga, well, let's split this shit up now, and we need to get started; the clock is tickin', shit, I'll hit you up later, bro said Jamal. The two friends slapped each other up, and Jamal called Kiesha while he was on the road to let her know he was on his way home. '' Daddy is missing his wifey and my pussy, we have business to discuss, but first, Daddy is coming home to take care of you baby''. Oh, Daddy, I'm ready for some back shots tonight; I have your drink and weed already prepared, baby.'' Bet I'll be there in 10.

When Jamal arrived home, he did his routine check around the perimeters of their house; He wasn't crazy. He knew niggas would try to take a nigga out while he was walking right into or leaving his house. Jamal was greeted by Kiesha wearing a pair of his boxers and one of his white tees, nipples hard as fuck. ''Dam baby, you make that shit look good as fuck as he looked at her assumable. Kiesha said as she handed him his drink, 'give me the bag, Daddy. Pleasure now, business later, correct?

She turned around to put the bag on the floor and to walk into the bedroom; the view that Jamal had was wonderful; every time she took a step, her ass checks jumped, and so did his dick. Kiesha, who was freshly showered and smelled good, slipped out of the boxers and white tee, only leaving a red pair of heels on. She loved riding his dick with her heels on, walking towards the bed with the sexiest walk. She pushed play on the radio and the music of P*$$Y Fairy (OTW) by Jhene, Aiko, filled the room.

The light was dimmed, and she lit a blunt for them to share; once it was lit, she took a pull on the blunt and blew it in his mouth as he held on to her ass. Doing a partial split on his dick, she started riding him reverse cowgirl style. She took the time to look at him over her shoulder, letting him know that he was hitting all the right spots. Passing the blunt back and forth, the couple was feeling real nice this night. Kiesha got up on her knees and lifted her ass in the air; Jamal took his thumb and started caressing her asshole; yeah, she knew what time it was. She knew what daddy wanted. She took one final pull from the blunt and passed it underneath her and Jamal caught it from the back of her with his left hand.

Blunt in the left hand, Dick in right hand, Jamal was looking down to see how he was carrying his tools; he started to spread Kiesha's ass and slowing rub his dick right between her ass, "daddy, take it, baby, take ya, ass baby". With that command, Jamal entered her from behind and let out a cloud of smoke. "Ahhh shit baby, fuck this ass feels good, slap... slap… is all you heard as their skin was vibrating together to the same beat. Cum in yo ass daddy, oh shit baby, who am I daddy, who am I? Yo you, my fuckin wife, shit Kiesha FUCK!!, I'm about to nut as his speed grew faster. She was taking them back shots like a fuckin pro. They both came simultaneously.

Dam, Daddy, that shit was good as fuck; join me in the shower? Hell yeah, Jamal replied as he slapped her on her ass, now nigga you can leave her alone for the rest of the night. They both laughed. After the shower they gathered the black bag and went into the office to discuss business. Alright, babe, altogether, we have twenty bricks. I split that shit like this; you have 7 ½, I have 6 ½, and D has 6. Do you think you can handle it between here and the falls?" "Hell yeah, shit, just in the Falls, I can drop 3 with my people. What's are turn around looking like? Shit, a week, you cool with that. Jamal asked.

Yeah, I should be good, Daddy; let me call as she pulls out her work phone. "What's the ticket? The voice said. Three for 60, but I'll let it go for 55 for you. Thanks, tomorrow morning I'll come to you she said. She drops the phone into a glass of champagne. Who the fuck did I create EL Chapo Jr, babe? Jamal laughed at his comment. Baby, you worked that shit out quick, "shit Daddy, thanks, yes you taught me well, and you taught me never to leave a trace that could lead back to us. "I'll handle what I need to up there, and then my peoples down here can do the rest; what about you, are you straight?

She asked. "Yeah, I'm good; I called on the way home. This shit is for life," they said together and sealed it with a kiss. Now business was complete; they fucked each other good, and nothing was left but to crawl in bed together to watch reruns of their favorite show Sons Of Anarchy.

CHAPTER 11

Girl, get up. I have something to tell you, Monica said to her friend over the phone. ''Where's Mal? Bitch I'm at your front door. ''Come on in. I'm about to get up. The door will be open, I'm about to buzz you in. Kiesha got up, threw on a pair of sweatpants and a T-shirt, and pulled her hair up in a ponytail. What's up girl, you good? Kiesha asked her friend as she walked down the hallway stairs to her best friend because it wasn't like Monica to pop up since she had moved in with Jamal.

Girl, hell yeah, I'm good. ''Sooo I was out at the bar last night because you didn't answer your phone, and I ran into Dale'. ''Yeah and'? Kiesha said. Then she looked at Monica and yelled, ''Bitch you fucked Dale!!!''. Monica busted out laughing, ''Bitch I rode that dick all night, they slapped each other up. ''Shit, if I would have known he was packin' like that, I would have been gave his ass some when he was trying to talk to me at the bank, but shit, better late than never.

''I knew it bitch. I watch his ass with you; he's very attentive to you, best friend, all shit go head bro Kiesha said smiling.

Yeah, I've always thought that he was cute and shit, but I normally don't talk to my coworkers or clients at the bank; but ever since I switched branches, that nigga been looking hella fine."

"So, you know ain't no other bitch coming here with him no more, right?" replied Kiesha. You're right, girl. He just doesn't know it, but he's about to home for a bitch.

"Nigga you fucked Monica, nigga. When? Where? "Shit nigga after you left my crib, I went down the way, and she was out by herself. We got to talking, and drinks started flowing. Plus, I've been trying to holla at Monica for years, but she never would cross that line from business to bae". "That's my nigga, now maybe you two can focus on each other when we're all out together instead of me, and the Mrs. Jamal said, laughing. "Fuck you nigga Dale said, laughing alongside Jamal, now let's hit up our people, its money out here to be made.

Back at the house, Kiesha asked Monica if she wanted to ride to the falls with her. Business or pleasure chick? Monica asked. Business, and before you say anything, I have it covered; nobody is going to find anything if we get pulled over, Kiesha told her. Shit, we better not; a bitch can't get the good dick if I'm locked up with yo ass," Monica replied. "Good, let me go and get dressed, yo ass come over here looking like a Victoria's Secret fuckin model and shit".

Kiesha came from her bedroom looking fine as hell with a crop top & matching skirt and a pair of 7-inch red bottoms heels. Her hair was bone straight with a Chinese bang, and she was feeling herself. ''Let's roll chick''. Bumpin the music of Hair Down by SiR, they took a quick trip to Niagara Falls. One they arrived, the words ''Dam Kiesha, you lookin real good there baby'' came from Kiesha's business partner in crime. She had only known Main for about 8 ½ months after meeting him one night at a club in the falls, but the business bond that they had formed was turning into a solid one.

''Alright nigga keep that shit to yourself, Main; I told you I'm already taken. The two embraced each other. ''Shit, my bad, Kiesha, a nigga can't help himself, but if you ever get tired...STOP RIGHT THERE!! Disrespect him, and you disrespect me. ''Ok, ok, much respect, miss lady, let's get down to business; Monica looking good as usual'. Thanks, boo! They all went into Main's office.

Dam Kiesha, where does this shit come from? Main took a quick sniff to test the product. ''Fuck, this shit is pure as fuck, he said as he wiped his nose and his watery eyes. 55, right? Yes, sir, but I have three more for a total of 6 for $115, ''shit word'? He asked. Yeah, but if we're going to do that, then I need to come back tomorrow. Or I could come to you and meet your connect; we could always do that, Main said.'' Kiesha turned to look at him and said now you know I don't conduct business like that nigga; this shit is strictly between you and me. ''Shit, you can't be made at a nigga for trying, but most respect Kiesha, I love your hustle. I'll be right back. I know you don't stay long; let me get yo bread. Thanks, Main. He came back into his office with $55,000 for her. I'll have the rest by the time you arrive tomorrow. Perfect, thanks, Main; it's always a pleasure. I'll hit you up tomorrow before I come.

She and Monica finished saying their goodbyes and hopped back in the car. In less than 40 minutes, Kiesha had sold all her shares of the bricks except for a small portion. A pretty face and a strong business mind were all she needed, she thought.

1/2 Left daddy omw home baby, I fuckn love you.'' "Alright, nigga, finish breaking that shit down. We need that shit cut twice; a nigga is trying to have a little extra. BUZZ, Jamal looked at his phone, noticing he had a message from Kiesha, and he picked it up to read it. YOOOO, my boo did her mutha fuckn thing''. There was no need to text back; he knew her business cell phone was already destroyed, and he did the same once he read the message. Once the ladies arrived back in Buffalo, they decided to do some shopping and go out to lunch, ''dam girl, you must be feeling Dale, shit you've been on your phone since we got back on the road'.

''Yeah, I ain't gonna lie, girl, I've always had a thing for him, but I already knew how work relationships go, and my job means everything; he's always been respectful and cool as shit, but with him hanging around now so much because of Jamal, I could definitely see myself booed up with him." 'That's what's up, sis, shit. You can tell he's feeling you, too; I wish you all the best of luck. All my bro and sis, I love are little family. Couples' dinner tonight? Asked Kiesha. I'll tell Jamal and you hit up Dale.

Jamal and Dale were busy making deals, visiting stash houses, and finding new runners when they both got the text about date night. Even though Jamal wanted to finish his business, he loved Kiesha so much; the world was hers, so if she wished to date night then so be in. "Yeah, it looks like they've been talking Jamal said, laughing; oh, I see you got the same message Dale said, holding up his phone to Jamal. A text was sent back to make dinner reservations for 9:30, somewhere romantic. Jamal said I want to spoil my wife tonight.

Kiesha said shit; I'm glad we went shopping; my man is pulling out all the shits tonight; girl, you can use the spare bedroom to shower and get dressed; I'm about to make the reservations and then start getting myself ready. Kiesha was looking through the new things she had just purchased. She chose a red bra and crotchless panty set to wear underneath. She was followed by a red wrap-around skirt with a slit right up to the panty line and matching top. It was a ponytail night; he loved pulling her hair in the bedroom. She wanted Jamal to have a full view of what he was getting when he got home, shit maybe at the restaurant, as she looked at herself in the mirror while adding perfume onto her body. Monica decided to wear a blue satin shirt dress that would flow perfectly while she was on the dance floor. Perfectly fixing her beautiful short pixie cut, she looked at herself and said damn, I'm fine as hell as she slapped herself on the ass.

Dale and Jamal stopped by Dale's house for him to shower and shave as Jamal asked Kiesha to have his clothes out for him. Dale steps out in a pair of blue jeans with some Tims and a matching blue jean jacket with a black shirt underneath. Dale was chocolate with a bald head and a beautiful physique; he stayed in the gym and kept his beard trimmed, but not too much, because he knew the women loved pulling on his beard. Once he was done, they headed over to Jamals for him to get dressed.

Hey, daddy, Kiesha said, how did everything go? ''Shit, we straight, Baby, you look beautiful Jamal said. I see you did well; I'm going to have to go next time to see who this nigga is that's doing business with my wife. ''No sir, remember I handle my business by myself, and then I come home to handle you she said with a wink'. ''Yeah, you better be handling some shit tonight; my dick has been jumping all day, baby. Grabbing his dick, she said oh don't worry, he's going to be taken care of; now go and get in the shower so that we can go.

" Dam Monica, I see we think alike looking at the colors chosen; you look good as hell, girl. Thanks, you clean up well yourself. Dale leaned in to kiss Monica; you aren't got any fuckin panties on, boo? he asked when he went to cup her ass as they kissed; she licked his lips, round 2 baby, on the way. "Shit, them niggas can drive in their car. We need some alone time, A yo Kiesha; we will meet you all there'. Yeah, ok, nasty asses, lol; just be careful.

Pulling off to Show Me, Love, by Alicia Keys blasting through the speaker, Dale, and Monica left to go to the restaurant. So "what's up with round two? Miss no panties". "Shit, you tell me Monica said as she took his hand and ran it up her dress. As soon as his fingers reached her freshly shaven pussy, he instantly started finger fuckin her as she lifted her leg onto the dashboard for him to have better access. That shit feels good. Baby, he asked yes. Yes, deeper D, deeper. He liked her calling him D. After her second time coming from his magical fingers, she unzipped his jeans and took all 8 ½ inches of him into her mouth. GOT DAMMMM Girl, Fuck!!!

She fed off of his dick until he came right on time as he pulled over on the side of the road. She played Chris Browns New Flame on the cars radio, and she climbed on him backwards to the point where his dick was hitting her G spot, drive she requested; Dale put the car in drive, and with every bump in the road, his dick was going deeper and deeper inside of her. WTF, baby he said, is this what the fuck I've been missing as she rode him while he was riding the road. SHHH, she said, speak when you're spoken to, she pushed his foot on the pedal to speed their speed up. Oh, oh fuck D, fuck this pussy baby, she bounced and bounced until his dick was covered in her creaminess. This shit is mines, you better not give this pussy, my pussy away, do you fuckin hear me he said.

They came just as they were pulling up to the restaurant; they both headed to the bathrooms to clean themselves up. We aint staying long; shit, I aint done with yo ass he said. Dam, where you niggas been? We have been here for a short waiting on y'all Jamal said. Business nigga business Dale, said as he slapped Jamal up. Let's order a nigga starvin.

The couples ate, drank, and danced. The ladies were grinding all over their men, and Kiesha said follow me, baby, as they crept off to the women's bathroom. Bending over the sink so she could see them in the mirror, Jamal looked at the red crotchless panties and said dam, my favorite color. Her pussy lips were busting through the opening of the panties glistening from all her wetness. He spread her ass and made love to her as they both looked straight into each other's eyes through that bathroom mirror that night. The couples were all fucked out, and they were ready to retrieve to their homes for some much-needed rest.

CHAPTER 12

911…911, Dale, Jamal, and Kiesha's business phones were going off. They all knew that meant trouble and to get to the main stash house. Everyone, including Monica, jumped up to get dressed and head out. WTF happened, Jamal said as he entered the house, the smell of burnt flesh and shit hit their nose. Someone had killed two of their best runners and stole the dope. FUCK!!!!!! They both said as they looked at everyone, somebody better fuckin says something. One of the young boys said "man, all we know is all last night we heard niggas that aint from around here asking about the dope and where it came from, and I was calling these niggas to give them a heads up, and they weren't answering so we came over and seen this shit.

Mutha, fucka, you didn't think to call my phone then instead of now? Jamal said. I didn't want to bother you, big dawg; oh, you didn't want to bother me? Dale, you hear this shit, the nigga didn't want to bother us, yeah, I hear the little nigga, he didn't want to bother us about our dope and niggas lurking, dam that's crazy. "But I did hear…Dale put two to the back of the nigga head. "Nigga WTF D, Jamal hollered;

nigga he was about to talk; wtf is wrong with you, D? We don't do business like that". "Man, that nigga was just wasting time, he ain't know shit. Fuck that nigga ".

Yo, D. we're fucked that was all the money that we had tied up in this shit. That nigga from Miami will have niggas looking for us. Light this mutha fuckin up, and let's go before the police get here, Dale said, and just like that, the house was in flames, three dead runners and any evidence went with them.

I'll meet you all back at the house, Jamal said to Dale and Monica; as they were driving, Dale looked at Monica and said you well, baby? Are you good, babe? She looked so shaken up; he looked at her and said Monica, I love you, but if you can't handle my life, let me know now. She leaned over the seat, kissed him, and said I love you too. Back at the house, they all sat in the office trying to figure out who, what & how.

"Yo nigga, who in the fuck is trying us? This shit can't go unhandled, Dale. Them niggas from Miami will have our fuckin heads nigga; we have no product, no money WTF." Mal, calm down, Kiesha. He asked her how much do you have? Just ½.I already sold my people in the falls the other three, but that's still nowhere enough, babe. "FUCK!!!! Jamal said, pounding his fist on the desk. "Yo, we need another plan. We have five days left to be back in Miami, and if we're not, then we better be ready for war. We need niggas ears to the streets, niggas here startin' to think we pussy nigga, whoever did this shit was trying to make a point. Jamal said. Yeah, we just took a major loss, and this shit will not go unanswered; D we need to pull all of our runners off the street and see who knows what; somebody is going to pay for this shit, real talk." Let's go to the rest of the stash houses and pull all the money and see what we got; this shit just got real D. "Shit, bet, let's go and meet back up here in an hour, stay safe. Monica was sitting back in surprise, watching all of this unfold before her eyes. She knew her friend was down with Jamal's business, but she had no idea how deep she was in.

"Yo, Bro, this shit is bad, nigga. I was just about to call you; these niggas hit the spots over here, too. Somebody dying tonight niggas is fuckin with business real talk nigga, but they to pussy to step to us. Meeting ASAP at the house, everybody, Jamal said.

"So, what's left? We need to find a plug down here; Kiesha has a short left, and there are 6 in the safe downstairs. "Lucky, Mone, did you niggas have a chance to re-up" Jamal asked their top two runners. "Naw, big bro, these niggas took the dope, money; shit, they even took the fuckin scales. ManMan, the other runner said "shit, same here". Fuck we are still almost $200,000 short, and we need that shit like yesterday he's expecting us back in a couple of days.

CHAPTER 13

Baby, can I talk to you? Kiesha said. Yo, we will be right back. Kiesha had a suggestion, and she was hoping her man was on board. ''Baby, I think I have a way to get us out of this situation but promise me you will hear me out.'. ''Ok, I trust you, babe, what's good, a nigga is a little stressed right now. ''Wait right here, I'll be right back'. She goes into her closet and comes back out with a safety deposit box. ''Shortly after my mom died, a guy came to my house and gave me an envelope; the envelope was from my mom''; she opened an account under a different last name and left me this''. She pushed the box towards Jamal; confusion was all over his face.

As he opens the box, Kiesha says I didn't tell you about it because she didn't want anyone to know about the money; she just wanted to ensure that I was taken care of'. ''Wait, so I don't take care of you?'' You didn't feel like you could fuckin trust me? Have you been hiding this in the house all this fuckin time, Kiesha? ''Baby, I just told you why I did it, but I'm giving it to you now so that we can get out of this shit; I'm sorry that I kept this from you, baby. I'm so sorry as she started to cry.

''Don't cry, babe, but I don't want any secrets between us; besides you, D is the only person that I fuckin trust with everything. I will always be there for you, but there must be absolutely no secrets.' Dam, but for real, how in the hell did you hold on to all this cash, with your shopping spree having ass? He asked her as he laughed'. ''Shut up,'' Kiesha replied with a smirk as she was wiping her tears. I'm serious, babe; take this money and get us out of this shit and let's start to rebuild again'.

Let's go and let everybody know; we are about to make some major fuckin moves. Thank you, baby, thank you, Jamal said. As they returned to the office, D was on the phone talking to someone, but he hung up when they entered. ''Yo, what up bro, who was that? Shit, I was trying to see if anyone had heard anything, its crickets out there, my nigga; who's ever behind this has some fuckin pull out here in these streets because ain't no one talking. ''Yo, we about to be back on, no questions asked, but my baby girl just hooked us up, so y'all need to stay here tonight, get some sleep, and we will put together a plan early in the morning'. Monica looked at Kiesha because she knew her friend and how much her friend loved Jamal, and that could only mean one thing: her friend gave her life's savings away. Kiesha just shrugged her shoulders at her friend.

As I said, my sis is a ride or die; love you, sis D said, Love you too, bro. That night it was different for them all; everyone was in their world; D kept getting text messages on one of his phones, ''Listen nigga if that's another bitch, let me know because I'm with the shits to bust a bitch upside her head.'' Calm down, Monica; I already told you it's you and me; this is all business over here (as he held up his phone). ''Yeah, it better be she said as she kissed him on the lips; shit spread them other lips, he commanded, a nigga a little hungry tonight.''

Yes, babe, your wish is my command, as she laid on her back and arched it with her legs open. While there was fuckin going on downstairs, Jamal and Kiesha were holding each other on once again a newfound bond they were creating. ''Baby, thank you again; you helped a nigga out''; Shit, D and I would be two niggas lost right now''. You're welcome, and baby, it's us against them. Besides, you have taken such good care of me, Daddy, and I want to help us out. ''So, what's the full story with you and D? How long have you all been cool?

''Shit, I meet that nigga like nine years ago. When I was in Memphis, I got real tight with the nigga; he showed me from day one he was loyal. He was making trips to Buffalo long before I came here; shit, he's the one that persuaded me to come here. He came up here looking for his father after his mother died, He was also trying to make his moves, and since we were connected in Memphis, it wasn't too hard for me to say no when he asked me to make the move here; then after I did the nigga moved to Dunkirk Jamal said laughing. He didn't have too much information about his dad, so he looked for a while, and then he just stopped looking and never mentioned the nigga again. All I know is that ever since I met him, he's been down, and I trust that nigga with my life, but like anyone else, he has his secrets but there his not mines to figure out.

CHAPTER 14

How the fuck is that possible'' David was asking the person on the other end of the phone. ''Yeah ok, I trusted you to get the information I needed. This nigga has to have a past, and I'm not happy with no bits and pieces of information. How fuckin hard can it be to look into a nigga? David was hanging up the phone as Knock entered the room. So, the little nigga fucked it up, huh boss? Bro, something in my gut is telling me to watch this nigga Jamal, and you know how I get when it comes to my gut; there's something there, I just know it.''

''Shit, you need me to holla at the nigga for you. I can get some information out of him real fast, fuck no; I don't need my daughter being hurt anymore than she already has, especially since she told me he proposed to her. ''Yeah, alright, boss, I'm just looking out for you. ''Much appreciated, my nigga, I'll let you know when you're needed. Yo, send that shorty in here for a while, I need to let off some steam before I go home. Mia is starting to get on my fuckin nerves.

"Hey Papi, you need me? Said the 5'4, 135 lb. Puerto Rican & half Dominican girl who was friends with Knocks girl. She had long black hair, thighs, and ass that went on for days. She loved walking around in booty shorts and heels every day. David had his eye on her for quite some time. "Hell, yeah shorty, what's up with you lately? You be around here showin' that ass like you want a nigga to touch it. Is that what you want? "Shit nigga, you late as hell; if you couldn't catch the fact that the pussy was coming your way, maybe I'm barkin' up the wrong tree".

Why don't you let you let "Thickness come over there and show you what you've been missing'. Thickness huh? Bring your ass here with yo fine ass. Thickness sat all her ass right on Davids's desk and propped her foot up between his legs, dam baby, I see you workin' with something, shit you thought I wasn't, David replied". She hopped down off the desk and right to her knees; David turned the music of Nipsey Hussle's I Don't Give a Fucc up in the office because he was about to let the stress of the phone call he just had, Mia and everything else out and no one needed to hear that.

"Dam shorty, you suckin' this dick like yo life depends on it, Thickness started to come up off the floor to stand up, but she was pulling and rotating his dick at the same time. "Fuck girl, dam, and just as she came up to the top of his head and her heel touched the floor, her mouth slid back down on his dick to his balls... FUCKKKK, he let out. She continued to do her tricks all over his dick until he pulled her up, slapped on a rubber and threw her leg up on the desk, and fucked the shit out of her, pounding her ass to where she thought her back was about to brake, but she took that shit like a G.

As he started to cum, she flipped herself over on the desk and said, oh no, Papi, I know what you feel like; now I need to know what that nut tastes like, she slid the condom off his dick with her mouth, and she finished what she had started and sucked his dick until he came. ''Until next time Papi', as she wiped her lips, shit hell yeah, he replied.

A morning text came through to Kiesha ''Hey baby girl, how are you and your guy doing? Hit me back and let me know you ok is what she was awakened to. Were good pops, and you? They had an excellent relationship, but it seemed like ever since the lunch date at the pool hall the energy shifted, and she wasn't feeling that. Maybe it's Mom or the new chick; maybe it's the pool hall, but something is up with my pops. I hope he's ok, she thought to herself. She gets up and joins Jamal in the downstairs office to discuss their next moves, using the connect.

''Hey, babe, my peoples in the Falls want to know what's up with some extra product, dam babe, is this nigga using this shit for personal use, or is he moving this shit in the streets? Jamal asked Kiesha. Babe, does it matter? If the nigga is buying it up, does it matter what he's doing with it, husband? The look Jamal gave Kiesha said Fuck yes, it does. She left that question alone.

OK, so what's the plan, babe? Are you and Dale going back to Miami, can I come with you this time? Yes, babe, we're going, but I need you to stay back here and keep an eye on shit for us. I promise we will take a trip there, just the two of us real soon." We're going to pay the nigga there and bring back what we can and finally get business back to where we should be; we leave tomorrow morning. They spent the rest of the day with the two of them, loving each other and planning their future wedding day.

The following day, Dale came to pick Jamal up to head to the airport. On the way there, Jamal asked him, "Bro, you good. You seem to be somewhere else this morning, and I need you to be in the right headspace when we hit Miami. "Yeah, I'm good nigga just thinking about some shit, but I promise you my head is straight. Let's go and make this shit happen. Jamal accepted his friend's answer out loud but quietly; he was still suspicious. Something was bothering his friend, but he knew Dale well enough not to pry. That following day, they were back on that plan, heading back to Miami. The two friends were lucky as hell to have the TSA agents at the Buffalo airport and the Miami international airport in their pockets, which allowed them to be able to bring the drugs back.

Back home in Buffalo, Kiesha was rockin' shit out; she made a vow to have as much of the product gone by the time Mal and Dale came back home. Shit, let me go and do one final round-up before I go in tonight, Kiesha thought to herself. She called one of their soldiers to do the run with her because she knew better than not to have someone with her than to be out there alone. She and Lee were on their last pick up when they heard something creeping in the back room; looking at each other, the street runner drew his gun and motioned for her to stay back. As he slowly approached the back room where the noise was coming from, he had his rifle ready to unload on anyone who wasn't supposed to be back there. Instantly, Kiesha heard the commotion and ran towards the back; that's when she heard one shot. "Lee! Lee!" she started running towards the back. Lee said I'm good boss, I'm good, but this nigga ain't, as he began to kick whoever the thief was.

WTF is going on. Boss lady, somebody is targeting our operation. "Fuck this nigga"!!! as he shot the nigga again. "I need to call Jamal, we gotta clean this shit up now and get the fuck outta here' 'Kiesha said as she started dialing Jamal's number from her regular phone.

"Hey, babe, what's good love? Babe, hello? He said again. Hey baby, I was wondering when you were coming home because your investment didn't go as planned, and I need your help'.

Jamal sat up in the bed because he knew she was talking in code, and something was wrong.

"Ok, babe, can you handle it until tomorrow? We arrive first thing in the morning?", are you ok?

I'm good, babe. Trust me, it's nothing I haven't handled before. Right then and there, he knew what she was saying, and he headed to Dale's room to let him know what was happening. As much as he wanted to get more information from Kiesha, he knew that they couldn't say too much on the phone. Lee was doing what he needed to do, which was to protect Kiesha; he had already started the cleanup process and was preparing to get her back home with no traces of them being at the stash house.

Jamal sat in Dale's hotel room, filling him in on what he could, and they prepared for their departure back home. They had already handled their business, but they knew there was no time for playtime, and they were headed back home to some unfinished business.

CHAPTER 15

Another one? Jamal said once he returned to Buffalo, this time without Dale, who went home to Monica. Yo, this shit stops here. I'm about to start hitting everybody's block until I find who the fuck is responsible, Fuck this shit. ''Calm down baby, we handled that shit before he was able to take anything, and we got rid of anything that could lead back to us''. Kiesha said to him. Did you or Lee recognize the nigga? No, he wasn't from here, babe, but I promise you we didn't leave anything behind, so I need you to calm down Jamal''.

''That's not the fuckin point, Kiesha; it's the fact that somebody is targeting us; it's like they know our every fuckin move''. Who he fuck are you cussing at, Jamal? This is not us, so let's not start turning on each other now. I'm sorry, baby; it's just that I feel like lately we are getting ambushed. I will never disrespect you again, the love. I am genuinely sorry. He bent down and kissed her on her lips.

The cops are going to start putting two and two together, bodies coming up missing, fires and break-ins; somebody has it out for us, and I won't stop until I find the person responsible for this.

Jamal told Dale what his next moves were and that he would need his full attention. He understood that Monica and Dale were vibing, but he couldn't allow Dale to lose control. Just a button on repeat, Dale and Monica were following Kiesha and Jamal's footsteps; not a night went past without them being together. Monica and Dale fell hard for each other, but Jamal had never been so focused on anything in his entire life. The more Dale fell in love with Monica, the more he fell back away from his business operations with Jamal.

Bro, I need you tonight Jamal said to Dale over the phone. What up bro, what's good? ''Nigga I'm putting some new runners to the test, and I need you to watch my back, same ole shit nigga''. ''Man bro'', ''no nigga don't man bro me Jamal said. I need you, D. You're the only one besides Kiesha I trust, but she's never done this, so I need you to be my extra eyes nigga''. Dale knew his friend was right: Dale knew his friend was right, I got you. I'll be down there soon'. Bet, meet me at my crib, we can ride together.

Once Dale was down in Buffalo, he pulled up to Jamal's house, ''I have to talk to my brother. I know he feels like I'm pulling back. Jamal came out of the house and jumped in the car with Dale. ''What up, bro? Jamal said as he slapped Dale up." Shit, nothing, so tell me who these new niggas is, and where did you find them at? Our little homie Slick found them on the west side, these little niggas trying to make a name out here for their selves, so he brought them to us. Let's just see how book-smart and street-smart these niggas are, and then we can see where or if we can use them in our operation.

''Yo have you heard anything from the connect in Miami, I've been calling the nigga, and he ain't answering Jamal said. Shit, I haven't heard from that nigga since the last time we were there, but I'll hit him up. Yeah, because if the nigga ain't fuckin with us, then we have to move on. ''Shit, we brought him his money back with intrest so I don't see what the issue could be,'' Dale said as they were pulling up to the new location of the stash house.

''What up, little homie they both said to Slick, one of their up-and-coming runners. Slick was 17 and had been with them for the last year; every chance he got he was showing them his worth. Shit, nothing, just ready for you to check these niggas out. The nigga in the red shirt is Bone, and the nigga in the black shirt is T, Slick said. I went to school with them, I trust these niggas. ''Nigga we need to trust them first,'' Dale said ''now, just you bring them over here''.

A yo what up little niggas, what y'all little niggas trying to do? Dale asked. Man, we're just trying to survive, big dawg.''. Shit, we trying to be with y'all niggas; show us the way, T said to Dale and Jamal. First step was to see how the two young men did with weighing up the products, packing them, and last but not least making a couple of runs to see how they handled the streets. Dale looked at Jamal and said ''it's like looking at us all over again'. ''Right nigga, it's like looking in the mirror''. They both were very surprised at how much knowledge T and Bone had. See, sometimes the streets are just in you; you don't have to be taught, it's just who you are, and this was the case with these two.

Towards the night's end, everyone sat down to discuss today's activities. Listen, Jamal said, you all did alright, but we still can't put you all out there like that right away. Bone, you're going to be with Slick and T, and you're going to be with our man, Shawn. They made these decisions because they both felt T had more potential than Bone, so they wanted him with someone like Shawn, who would bring out the best in T. Shawn was one of the first runners to start with Jamal and Dale when they first set up shop in Buffalo. 'Let's see how shit goes for a week, you Lil niggas be safe out here; be back tomorrow by 7 am sharp. If it's 7:01 and you're not here, don't bother showing up.

CHAPTER 16

On the ride back, Jamal decided to talk with his friend. ''What's up, bro? You say you're here, but I know my brother, and you're not, so talk to me. '' Man, honestly, I will always have your back, but the night I bodied that nigga in front of Monica, I saw the fear in her, and I ain't trying to run shorty off Mal. I love her, but I don't think she's built for this man. I want to get out of the streets and build something with her. I've never felt like this before'.

''Oh shit, yeah nigga you got the love bug, I understand''. Nigga I know you ain't talking. Kiesha got yo ass on lock; they both started laughing. But real talk, Mal, do you ever think you will get out of the game and go legit? No, this is who I am, and I've found someone to accept this part of me.'' I respect that, bro, but it's time for me to find another path and take my lady with me'.

Alright, let's do this last run together; the nigga that's been blocking us has gotten lucky, so it's finally time for us to come up and get back at him. So, in two days, we will pull these deliveries off, and yo ass can go into retirement Jamal said to Dale. ''Bet is everything set; everybody knows their role to play asked Dale' 'ready as they will ever be." The ride ended, and the two friends went their separate ways, preparing to finish what they had started together.

The next night, Slick was watching over the stash house with T; he knew he had to guard the product with his life. Sitting in the house, T said he was getting ready to walk to the store; shit cool, I'm about to go and take a shit nigga. Remember, always watch your back and go and come right back. There has to be two of us at all times; Slick said as T walked out the door to the store. Tee ran into a chick he had been feeling, and they started talking.

As Slick exited the bathroom, he heard someone rambling in the back room. Slick or T never knew they were being watched. He pulled his gun out and started making his way towards the noise. When he entered the doorway, he saw the nigga from the back loading up the product. Nigga drop that shit, or I will put two in the back of your fuckin head. The man held his hands up, and when he turned around, Slick said'' oh shit, what are you doing? I ain't know.

Those were the last words he got out before his body hit the ground. The man continued to put the previous three bricks in the bag as he heard T running through the house, calling Slick's name. He made his exit out the back door. T said ''Fuck, this is bad, this is bad!!! When he went to look out the back door, he couldn't believe his eyes; he saw the shooter, and the shooter saw him.

T started gathering his shit and was preparing to get the fuck out of dodge.

These niggas are going to kill me; he blew up Bones's phone, who had it on DND. Nigga answered your phone as he repeatedly called and text his friend, but Bone was laid up with his baby mama without a care in the world. T went straight home to pack a bag and hit the streets; he knew that if he was caught, he was a dead nigga. While packing his clothes, he went into the closet to grab some money he had stashed; he never saw it coming.

His killer knew that he had to go because letting him live, even for one more night, would have ended everything that they had worked so hard for, and that wasn't an option.

CHAPTER 17

Fuck me, D, Fuck me, baby, omg baby, what's up with yo ass tonight? Monica asked D as he was fucking her like never before. ''Oh, now you wanna run from the dick? Bring yo ass here he said to her as he pulled her ass back down on his dick; where the fuck do you think you are going? He was slapping her on her ass so hard, but she was loving every bit of it. ''Baby, I'm cumin, I'm fuckin coming, baby, she hollered as he continued with one hard long thrust and let his nut right off into her.

As they lay in each other's arms, Monica asked D if everything was ok tonight with Jamal. ''Yeah, we talked, and my bro understands that I'm trying to get out of this lifestyle; I just want to be happy with you, baby, and I can't do that if I'm looking over my shoulders'. Monica sat up in bed and said, "Baby, why didn't you tell me you were having these thoughts? I accept you for who you are. ''I hear you, ma, but it's time anyway before I end up dead or in jail. You coming along sealed the deal for me, shit it's now or never'.

Monica looked at Dales's face, and he had a worried look all over him; she laid back down in his arms. She had started getting comfortable with his lifestyle, but at the same time, she was happy that he was making this decision. She never judged Kiesha for following in Jamal's footsteps, but she secretly knew she couldn't be that kind of woman to Dale. She leaned in to kiss him as they fell asleep together.

'' Mal, Mal wake the fuck up, Kiesha said as she was hitting Jamal on his back while he was sleep''. ''Babe, what's wrong'?

''T and Slick were found dead this morning'. Jamal jumped up. ''What?'' he grabbed the remote and turned on the TV to see the news of two young men found dead by gunshots over night. Jamal threw the remote on the floor, ''Yo babe, call D. I'm about to put some clothes on and call Bone.

Bone woke up to several 911 text messages from Tee and Jamal. He called T back, no answer and then he called Jamal. ''Nigga where the fuck you at?'' Jamal asked Bone. What the fuck happened at the stash house to Slick and Tee? Bone is going through his phone as he's reading his missed messages from Tee. ''Man, big dawg, I don't know. I was chilling with my shorty, and I had my phone turned off, but something is wrong this nigga was blowing my phone up''.

''Wrong? Yeah, something is wrong. ''The nigga is dead,'' Jamal said; him and Slick Jamal said, nigga turn the tv on''. Bones jumped to see his friend's name across the tv screen as one of the victims; it broke him. ''Yo, were coming to get you to send me the address; this shit stops tonight, niggas is getting bodied; fuck this.

"You just said you were done, D; wtf now you're about to participate in a fuckin war, " Babe, I know Jamal. He's about to flip on any nigga that ain't down with us, and I'm not losing my brother". Get dressed, and you can wait at the house with Kiesha.

The ride from Dunkirk didn't seem that long as Dale pulled up to Jamal's house. "Listen nigga before we start knocking niggas off, let's see what's up. The news said T was found at his momma's house, so you know their all over this shit; this wasn't just some nigga shot at a trap house, Dale said to Jamal. "D listen, we have been taking hits for a minute now; this shit is personal as fuck to me". As much as Dale wanted to back out, he knew his friend was serious, and it was time to put that work in and then he was out for good. No looking back.

For the next 72 hours, Jamal and Dale were on niggas necks trying to find out who hit the stash house and killed Slick and T, but no one had any fuckin clue; it was like this mutha fucka didn't exist. The girl that T was talking to at the store found Bone, and he took her to Jamal and Dale and said, "I was with T when he heard the shot come from the house; he dropped his stuff from the store and ran back to the house. That was the last time I saw him because I ran home'. "Fuck, my man is gone; we been homies since the sandbox". "Calm down nigga, don't make no fuckin scene. Keep your emotions in check out here' Dale said to Bone.

Jamal looked at Dale and said ''wait, so he was here and then went to his mom's house? This doesn't make any sense D'. Shit did that nigga try to rob us and get caught? But if so, then by who? Dale said ''hear me, bro, it's time to cut our losses and get the fuck out of Buffalo, we ain't no pussies nigga, but somebody is working against us, and now with the nigga getting bodied at his momma's crib, the police are going to be involved like a muthafucka.

They gave Bone strict instructions on not talking to the police and gave him some money to pass on to T and Slick's mothers for their burial. Nigga it's hot here. Ain't nothing we can do tonight, so let's go back to your crib. I'm sure Monica wants to spend more time with Kiesha tonight, and we can talk and come up with a plan, Dale said. Back at the house, Kiesha was racing her brain about everything that had taken place since she's been with Jamal; shit, it feels like I'm his bad luck charm girl'.

''Girl, you're not his bad luck charm, but honestly, sis, this might be a sign for him to get out; Dale has already decided to get out, but if this shit keeps happening, he will never be able to walk away'. I don't know, girl, but before she could finish her sentence, Jamal and Dale came through the door. Babe, can you make me a drink? "We need to figure some shit out. Kiesha and Monica got up to make some drinks for everyone, and then it was time to sit and devise a plan. " Hear me, Mal, when you came to Buffalo, it was to make a name for yourself but stay under the radar, and we've been able to do that. "But the bullshit that's been coming our way is going to give us the attention that ain't neither one of us looking for. Battling the niggas in the streets is one thing, but them and the police nigga I ain't trying to do life."

"So were just supposed to leave, let the business go? And what about Kiesha? She can't leave her pops'. Baby, I go where you go, this shit is for life Kiesha said. My father has chosen to continue building his life with this chick Mia; he will be fine; he's never in Buffalo anyways; shit, my mother died, and he didn't waste any time forgetting about her. "

If leaving Buffalo is what it's about for us to rebuild and start over, shit, let's do it and build somewhere else even bigger and better. "Girl, I love you more and more every day,' Jamal said to Kiesha as the four clicked their shot glasses together. Jamal and Dale entered the office, and Kiesha asked Monica to help her with dinner for the four of them. It had been a minute since the four of them were together, and Kiesha missed that. They really had become her only family and she didn't see her life without them. That night they put business to the side, and they were just four friends laughing and drinking and showing each other love.

CHAPTER 18

Weeks had gone by, and no one had been arrested for T and Slicks murder. The police only had one piece of evidence to share with the public, and it was a piece of a coat that had gotten snagged on the backdoor at T house; they figured the killer was in a rush because they didn't go back for it. It wasn't much to put out to the public. Without trying to, Jamal and Dale were bringing attention to their street runners who were getting caught up. They weren't talking, but the multiple arrests became terrible for business. '' Kiesha said to Jamal one night.'' Baby, so what do you want to do? You've come too far to stop; I get it Dale is done, but shit, I'm just now getting a taste of this shit for real'. Dam babe, I've created a monster, Jamal replied with laughter.

She got off the couch to sit on his lap, ''oh yes, baby, you have,' she said as she kissed him on his lips. ''But seriously, baby, I get it shit is tight right now, but what's keeping you here? Nothing, I can answer that for you'. Let's start over somewhere that nobody else knows us, we can build because we won't have to look over our shoulders, and I can really be out there running shit with you. Shit is hard now because sometimes I do worry about my dad, but shit, I'm not letting anything stop me, but a new city, new people equal new opportunities.

This shit has been in you since day 1; yo ass is way too comfortable in the street life, boo; that shit makes my dick hard. ''Really, she said as she pulled the thong she was wearing to the side, ''Show me, show me how hard that dick is for me''. Jamal took one last puff of his blunt and said ''shit say less'', he bent her over the chair he was sitting in and started rubbing his dick back and forth across her ass until his dick was rock hard. Kiesha looked over her shoulder at him and said ''Take it'; and that he did. Jamal slides his dick right between her ass checks and right into her pussy.' Ahh shit, baby, that pussy feels so fuckin good; he grabbed her hands and pulled them backwards to have a better grip on her; Dam Kiesha, this shit feels good, baby, push that ass back on that dick, Fuck!!! You like that shit huh? Do you? She said.

Hell, fuck yeah, do that shit again for me baby, and once again, Kiesha took her ass and slammed it right down on his dick, allowing her pussy to swallow his dick up whole. ''What, you thought this shit was Daddy? This is my dick nigga she said as she rotated her ass on his suffocated dick. She looked back once more as she caught Jamal biting his fuckin lip, and she knew he was ready. She pushed her ass on him completely, which caused him to let her arms go to grab her ass, but he was too late. It took two more times of all that ass bouncing on top of that dick before she heard him calling her fuckin name out as he let off his nut inside of her. As their session ended, he slapped her on the ass and said '' shit, where are you trying to move to? I'm going wherever that ass is going, baby''. Kiesha looked at him, and they both said simultaneously 'This shit is for life''.

CHAPTER 19

Kiesha and Jamal continued to stay focused on building their business together, with Dale doing his own thing gave Kiesha the opportunity to have more responsibilities; as they were still deciding on their next move, they understood that this move would have to be their last one for a while so everything was carefully thought out. Kiesha understood that her father would not be happy with her decision to leave Buffalo, but she was ready to tell him. She was a grown woman and had to follow her heart and her future husband.

One day, Kiesha was thinking, wow, things have changed so much, ''you never know where life will take you. I went from being a teenage graduate to building an empire with my soon-to-be husband. At the same time, she was also thinking, but I barely see my pops anymore, and this is one part of my life I would never be able to share with him. Yeah, things have changed but she was learning once again on how to be ok with change.

The business was still going, but not like it was before; the fact that the killer of T and Slick hadn't been found was making the public feel unsafe. The Miami connect had completely cut ties with Jamal and Dale because he wasn't trusting them as businessmen anymore. With business slowing down it was giving Kiesha and Jamal time to plan their wedding. Babe, can you believe it's been a year since you asked me to marry you? I wanted something big, but with everything going on, we can have a small wedding, Mal; I don't care anymore. I'm just ready to be married to you and become Mrs. Black. Hell, no babe, you're going to have the wedding you deserve.

Pick a date, baby, and I will make it happen for you he told her. For real, Mal, are you serious Kiesha said as she jumped up and started dancing. Yes, baby, I'm serious. You deserve it, and we need something good to go on in our lives. April 24th, Kiesha said. Dam, you picked that date fast, baby'. April 24th is my mom's birthday; hear me out, Mal. I will always miss her. We had a morning routine where we made breakfast together every day before I went to school. Getting married on her birthday, I can celebrate and honor her'; please, Mal, can we?

"Baby, I told you before I would do anything for you, which gives us five months. Wow, I'm going to be a married man." Shit nigga you been a married man; wtf are you talking about? Kiesha said jokingly to him. You right, you right Jamal said; Babe whatever you want, I'm down, and I will be right by your side to do whatever needs to be done for our wedding. Now go ahead and call Monica because I know you're dying to; he said as he walked past her and slapped her on the ass.

CHAPTER 20

Chick, it's about time. Monica said I love you girl. I'm so happy for you'. Thank you, sis; we need to start planning for real. Monica, I need all your help. Monica said girl, please fuckn around with me. I'll be right next to yo ass at the altar.

On one side, Jamal was doing his best to keep his business afloat, even with all the roadblocks that were still coming his way. He was trying to keep certain shit from Kiesha; he just wanted her to focus on planning their wedding even though he knew if she found out how bad shit was for them, she would be upset for him keeping that kind of secret from her.

With all the bullshit that was taking place in their operation, only certain connects were fucking with them, but not the heavy hitters that he needed. Meanwhile Davids's business has been running with no hiccups as always; even without him being in the States, shit was running smoothly. Dale was secretly building his and Monica's exit from the world. He knew to live a life without worries; he had to leave the Buffalo and start over. Monica was the first person besides

Jamal that really felt like family to Dale, and he didn't want to lose that. Kiesha was a happy soon-to-be wife planning her dream wedding. Monica was enjoying herself and trying to settle into her new life. Everyone was doing what they needed to do to survive on their own terms.

CHAPTER 21

So, he's from Memphis; the only survivor from his parents and his brother, nobody else? David asked Knock. Nothing much boss; he hangs with a nigga named Dale, but shit, there doesn't seem to be any information on him either". We've been low-key watching her and the nigga, but it's hard seeing that she's seen a lot of us before Scar.". David said,' I've only been around my daughter with this nigga a handle full of times, and I've never heard of a nigga named Dale. There are two ways to look at this, either these niggas ain't about much, and they're boring ass hell, or there is more to these niggas that they're keeping a secret, and secrets get niggas killed. My daughter is getting married in less than three months, and I'll be back in the States; she aint marrying this nigga until I know EVERYTHING!!! And he hung up the phone.

Omg, I'm not feeling well, Monica thought, could I? am I? I need to go and take a couple of tests before Dale gets home. I just can't be pregnant; what will he think if I am? Monica drives to the closet drug store and picks up a couple of pregnancy tests.

1.. 2.. 3..4, test all saying I'm having a baby, omg I'm having a fuckin baby (she picks up the phone to call Kiesha). ''Wait, she thought, I need to tell Dale first; what if he says he doesn't want a baby? I don't want anyone to know if I have an abortion; please, God, let him be happy, she thought to herself as she was rubbing her stomach.

Monica accepted a long time ago that she was in this world by herself. She was put into the foster system from birth, so she's always depended on herself. She stayed focused in school, and graduated with a 4.0 while working her ass off to reach her goals at work, but having a baby was the one thing she secretly always wanted. Come on, little one, let's make dinner for daddy and let mommy put something sexy on for daddy. Monica cleaned and cooked dinner and showered before Dale came back home. Dale walked in ''Dam baby, it smells good as fuck in here. What the hell are you cooking? At that time Monica stepped out in a sexy red lace matching bra and panty set with the chocker attached with a pair of heels to finish her look off.

Dale dropped his blunt, fuck boo, dam, you look good; ah shit it's going to be a good ass night tonight. Bring that ass here, boo. Monica seductively walked over to Dale and started kissing him on his neck; she knew that was his soft spot to get him started. As he starts rubbing on her ass, his fingers rotate to her outer thighs and then her inner thighs and right to her pussy.

Is this my pussy he asked as her juices were being soaked up by his fingers, is this daddy's pussy I said? Monica answered yes, the fuck it is (never taking her eyes off him). He found that shit sexy as hell. Standing there, he lifts her leg over his shoulder, and she feels the tip of the dick. Is this want you want, D? You want my pussy, baby? Shit, hell yeah, I do he said as he grabbed his dick and slid it into her pussy while holding onto her leg. He was hitting every angle inside of her while they were in this position, ''OMG God baby, take this pussy baby, show me you want it''.

Dale fucked her until she was begging him to stop, but he kept going until he came right inside her. ''Dam baby, we were supposed to be eating, and then fucking, the food is cold Monica said, laughing. ''Shit, you can't come out here looking like that and think a nigga ain't going to want to fuck''. Monica warmed up their food, and they sat down to eat, ''look at our asses sitting here naked chowing down; this shit good as hell, babe'. Thanks babe Monica, said.

After eating, they showered and were getting ready for bed. Monica said Baby, I have something for you, as she pulled out a box and handed it to Dale. She said I couldn't wait to tell you as Dale opened the box. Looking at the four positive pregnancy tests, Dale looked up at Monica.

'Pregnant? Babe you're pregnant; I mean we're pregnant? He asked hugging Monica. Yes, baby, we're having a baby. Are you happy? Hell, fuck yeah, I'm happy; shit, we're about to have a little fucking D running around this bitch. Or a little Monica, she said, laughing. She looked at Dale and said Baby, I've never been so fuckin happy in my life, and it's because of you. I love you. Dale rubbed her stomach and said I love both of y'all. You're changing me, Monica, and I love you for that.

Monica said "I can't wait to tell Kiesha she's about to be an auntie. With a slight paused Dale said baby, can we just wait to say to tell them; let's just keep this between us for a while. Let's enjoy our little family between the both of us. Of course, babe. We will tell them when the time is right, but right now, it's us against the world. Dale wanted to tell Jamal so badly, but lately he was battling with his own emotions because he was hiding a secret from Jamal. Jamal was his brother for life, but he knew this secret would tear their brotherhood apart.

CHAPTER 22

Monica and Dale spent all their time in Dunkirk, for the past three months. Every day, Monica talked to Kiesha on the phone. She wanted to share the news with her best friend, but she understood that Kiesha had her own bond with Jamal, and she wanted her and Dale's bond to be just as strong. 'What's up a chick? Do you want to have lunch today? Kiesha asked her friend. I feel like I haven't seen my sister in a minute; yo ass went out to Dunkirk and fell in love and forgot about a bitch". Monica replied hell yeah, girl, I miss yo ass, where do you want to go and around what time? I'm hungry as fuck; let's do Texas Roadhouse around 2 Kiesha said, I'll meet you there. After Monica got off the phone, she went to find Dale to let him know she was meeting up with Kiesha, and she needed to tell her friend. Three months had already passed, and Kiesha was getting married soon. She walked around the house looking for him and he was nowhere to be found. She ended up going into Dale's man cave. Dam babe, where are you? She thought to herself, looking out the window. When Monica turned around, one of Dale's drawers to his desk was slightly open.

She went to close it, and she came across something that horrified her; why in the fuck does he have a picture of Mrs. Robyn on his desk? She continued to open up the desk, and that's when she saw something that she wished she never in a million years would have seen. There lay a picture of Mrs. Robyn dead in her shop.

"Let me explain' 'was all she heard; she looked up and saw Dale standing in the doorway. Through her cries she said, "Why in the fuck do you have this? How do you know Mrs. Robyn, and why in the fuck do you have pictures of Mrs. Robyn's dead body". Dale started walking towards her. "Stay the fuck away from me and answer my questions, what the fuck Dale. "ANSWER ME!!!

"Baby, please, please stop crying, stop yelling; please, but Monica couldn't help it. She threw up in the garbage can next to her, and she passed out as Dale caught her in his arms. When she finally came to she jumped up, looking around the room, adjusting her eyes to the light, and looking to see where Dale was. Surprisingly, he was sitting at the bottom of the bed looking at her. She sat up and crawled to the other side of the bed as she started crying again. Who are you? What's going on? Babe, please talk to me.

Dale started crying." Babe, I'm sorry. I never wanted it to come out this way. I wanted to tell you, but then I started falling for you, and then you got pregnant; it just never was a good time. "TELL ME WHAT', what are you trying to tell me? I didn't know you knew Kiesha babe. I swear I didn't. I didn't know until the day you brought her to the party. ''How do you know Kiesha,' she asked him. He lowered his head ''Her father, our father,' he said in a low tone. WTF did you say. Did I hear you say our father nigga?''. Yes babe. Don't babe me shouted back to him.

Baby, please, let me explain. When I was growing up, I never knew my father; my mother always talked about this man who was terrible to her and never wanted anything to do with us. When she died, I started searching for him, and it took me less than a year to find him at the pool hall after my mom was gone. I had nothing, babe, nothing. I went to him expecting him to embrace me because he was my dad. That nigga looked at me and told me his wife and daughter could never know about me; he gave me a loan for $50,000 to get myself together. I was only 18, baby. The nigga loaned me money, my father, like I was just a nigga in the streets, he said, crying. I tried to reach out to him several times after that day, but he never loved me; he always praised Kiesha, but I was his first born. I would check up on him from a distance, watching him be a family man while I was trying to survive, which led me to move to Memphis. I knew I had the gift to hustle, so I took the money he loaned me and started making a name for myself.

That's where I met Jamal, he started making moves, and we just connected. ''Is your name even Dale? Monica interrupted him. He put his head down. Is your name Dale? she asked again. ''Brian, my name is Brian. I started using Dale once I moved to Memphis. ''Keep going,'' she said. Even with me making the moves that I was making, baby I would still reach out to my father, and he would always say if I needed a job as one of his street runners, WAIT!!!, wtf do you mean street runners? Mr. D owns a pool hall, and Kiesha's parents are some of the most respected people I know.

No, he isn't baby; he's a monster. I told you I would keep tabs on him, right? He was cheating on her, beating on her, and one day out of the blue, he somehow contacted me and told me it was time to pay back the loan he gave me'. I drove down here, and he gave me full instructions on what to do and how to do it, and he said I wouldn't owe him anything, plus he would give me extra. But baby, I didn't do it for the loan; I did it to get my father's approval.

Say it, she said; fucking say it, Dale; Brian, whatever the fuck your name is. Say what you did'. He paid me to kill his wife; Monica grabbed her stomach and let out a painful holler. He grabbed her as she started beating in his chest; what kind of sick person are you? Who did I fall in love with? You fell in love with me, baby. I swear I never knew she was your friend; the day you brought her to the party, when I turned around and saw my little sister standing there with you, my heart dropped. Baby, I didn't know as he cried with her.

This is too much to handle. Does Jamal know? No, he doesn't even know my real name and baby, you can never tell them.

I'm a dead man if you do. I can't keep this from her. She's my sister in every way that counts; you've been in her face; she loves you, Dale; they're supposed to be our baby's godparents. They still can babe; you don't have to say anything; it won't bring her back, please baby. Nigga we're in the fuckin wedding; were you going to stand up there with them knowing what you did? "Babe, I've been battling this ever since Mal proposed; I was hoping we would be gone before they got married. I know I can't go to the wedding. Our father will kill me on site". She slapped Dale so hard; is that all your worried about? What about the fucking fact you would be standing there next to the woman whose mother you KILLED!!!!

At that moment, Monica stopped and said "Wait, so Mr. D had Mrs. Robyn killed? Why? Why are you holding on to the pictures?" I don't know why he did it, but I told you he's a monster in the streets. Scar is ruthless as hell'. " What name did you say? Did you say Scar? Mr. D is Scar? Do you know the stories we've heard about the nigga Scar, and you're trying to tell me it's Mr. D?

Better yet, isn't this the nigga that Jamal has been trying to figure out who he was because he was fucking up all y'all business, and you knew all this time? Dale, Jamal will kill you if he finds out wtf". Scar wasn't fucking our business up. It was me, baby". I was trying to get Jamal to stop, hoping he would want to leave Buffalo and we all could have left together. ''So, you were the one hitting the stash houses? Did you kill T & Slick? Babe, like I said, I was doing all of this to protect us. If things had gone as I planned, our father would have never known about me being here, Kiesha and Jamal would have been married, and you and I would have raised our baby together. ''I grew to love Kiesha, and I am sorry for what I did, but I had no choice, Monica, I had no choice'. ''You always had a choice; you could have left us the fuck alone the night you met her. Instead, you betrayed her and moved right on into her life, and you're still holding on to Mrs. Robyn's pictures like some sick reminder'.

''I keep the pictures for my protection. If he would ever try to have me killed, at least I had proof, pictures, text messages, and money transfers. I needed to protect myself; that's the only reason I'm keeping them, baby, I swear. Whenever he's been around, I always find a way to leave because I don't know what he would do if he saw me. Monica started thinking about a couple of times David was around, and everyone was there except Dale; it didn't seem like a big deal because it wasn't like he needed to know David, so no one questioned Dale for not being there. When I'm down in Buffalo, I don't go in his neck of the woods, but also, because he's always out of town and no one else knows me, it's easy for me to move around down there.

But as I said, I was keeping them for protection. Once you told me about the baby, I thought it was finally time to get rid of them because I wanted to ask you to move back to Memphis with me, and I would never have to look over my shoulders. I'm ready to get my life together; that's why I have started pulling back from the business with Jamal, I don't have anyone else; I want our little family baby. Please give me that; don't take it away from me, Monica.

He went to touch her hand, and she jumped a little. She was in her thoughts. She loved Kiesha with all her heart; she was her sister. It took Kiesha forever to get out of that dark place. Did she want to be the one to put her back there, and then she had the father of her child? She didn't want her child to grow up without a father, but if the stories were true about the person behind the name Scar, she knew Dale was right; he was a dead man if anyone found out.

At that moment she realized her love and loyalty for Dale trumped her love and loyalty over what she had for Kiesha. She looked at him and said promise me you're done with this street shit, and we are going to raise our baby differently'. I promise, baby, I fuckin promise. He kissed her stomach and then kissed her. Shit, I was supposed to meet Kiesha for lunch, what time is it? Hand me my phone, I have to fucking cancel; I can't see her now.

She sent a text to Kiesha and told her she had an upset stomach and that she would make their lunch date up. Kiesha looked at the text message "wow chickyeah, ok, I hope you feel better, boo; love ya" was the text she sent back.

CHAPTER 23

Ah yo, babe, these niggas acting funny or what to you?'' Jamal said to Kiesha. Hell yeah, this is the third time Monica has stood me up, and I know Dale has put the business relationship on the back burner. We get married in less than two months; Fuck it, Daddy, let's invite them here for a date night, I can cook, and we can just chill and play some games and shit; I'm not taking no for an answer, she said.

She picked up her phone to send her friend a message. What up, chick. I miss my sister, and I really want to see you; we want to see y'all tonight for dinner and games, boo so what's up? Yeah, I know. I've been M.I.A but I promise I will talk to you tonight; we will be there, I promise. How's tonight around 8? Perfect I'll let Mal know.

After Monica got off the phone, Dale was standing there looking at her; Babe, I don't know if I can do this he said. Oh yes, you can, you've done it before. We can't keep putting them off; I don't know about Jamal, but that bitch ain't giving up, so we have to pull ourselves together. Plus, I can't keep hiding my pregnancy. "Will you tell her we're moving out of town soon," he asked. I don't know; I am breaking a bond with my sister. Not only am I lying to her about one of the biggest secrets that I know will destroy her, but I'm also building a life with the person who took her life from her. WTF are we doing, Dale she said while rubbing her stomach. Once we leave the city baby, we ain't coming back, he said to her.

While getting dressed, Monica was asking herself if she could really look Kiesha in the face and continue to keep Dale... Brian's secret up. Looking in the mirror at her stomach, she thought to herself, I'm doing this for our family baby while rubbing her stomach. I can't let them take your daddy away from us. The entire ride down to Buffalo was a quiet one for the first time between Dale and Monica; as they got closer, she said Babe, I can't. Let's turn back around.' 'I'm going to end up saying something. This is too much for me. Dale pulled over and held Monica in his arms. Baby, we got this. I know it's going to be hard, but we don't have a choice, and I promise right after the wedding, we the fuck out of here. I've been thinking a lot about that. Jamal or Kiesha is not going to let us miss the wedding, and I know Scar is going to shit bricks when he sees me, so we have to run right after they say I DO.

Tonight, we need to tell them we're leaving right after the wedding. Kiesha is going to be so upset with me, and I have to tell her about the baby." Dale said Babe, can I ask you something?'. Now that you know who I am, do you still feel the same way about having a baby with me? Dale, we made our baby out of love. There are so many questions that I have, but I saw what Kiesha went through; how could I do that to our baby growing up without a father? I could never, and Mr. D or Scar will kill you. I have to do what's best for our baby'.

They ended the conversation as they were pulling up to the house. Dam, chick, you are getting thick. What's up, sis? I've missed you, Kiesha said to Monica as she hugged her. What up, my nigga, the two friends said as they slapped each other up. Kiesha said shit, dinner is almost done, it's going to be a good night, babe roll up'. Dale glanced over at Monica, hey, sis, let me talk to you Monica said to Kiesha. They went into the bedroom as Dale and Jamal went into their own little bubble.

"Ok, girl, why do you look like this is about to be a serious talk Kiesha told Monica. 'I'm pregnant, 3 ½ months now Kiesha. I'm going to be an auntie; omg, I'm going to be an auntie? She jumped up and hugged Monica, bitch why didn't you tell me she asked as she started rubbing Monica's stomach. We just wanted to enjoy; you know, I don't have any family. I just needed this time to wrap my head around the fact that I would be a mom. Girl, I'm so happy for you; you deserve this. Kiesha looked at Monica's face. "Monica, I know you; this is one of the happiest times in your life. Why do you look so sad?"

"Nigga you're moving her to Memphis. That was all Dale and Jamal heard Kiesha saying as she left the bedroom. Jamal looked over at Dale and said "Nigga what the fuck is Kiesha talking about". I was going to tell you, Mal. "Monica is pregnant, and I want to raise our baby back in Memphis. Mal, I told you I was ready to get out of the game, and I won't be able to do that if I'm here. You know my dad was never there for me, and I want to be able to give my baby everything right from jump'. Monica crossed her eyes over at Dale, and he just put his head down.

Nigga I respect that D, but you could have told me. So, when are you all moving to Memphis? Jamal asked. Right after the wedding, Monica stepped in and said. Kiesha turned around with tears in her eyes. What?? Why so soon? Sis, I want to get settled in and find a Dr. there for me and the baby, find a house. I want to do everything before I get further along. Plus, you and Mal will be on your honeymoon, and you can always visit us.

Jamal took Kiesha into his arms. I understand that sis, I really do, and I'm truly happy for y'all, but I'm going to miss y'all. All three of y'all, Kiesha said with a smile. My nigga you already know I got you, Jamal said to Dale; you have been my day one from the beginning. Go raise my niece or nephew and show them a different way. "Bet big dog,' Dale said. Kiesha broke the emotional conversation; Shit, well, I guess all of us ain't drinking and smoking, but shit can we sit down and eat.

She looked at Monica and mouthed the words 'I love you' with a smile. Monica sent it right back, then excused herself to the bathroom, Dale followed her. Trying to muffle her cries in Dale's chest, looking at her best friends/sister; this shit was eating her up. Dale picked her head up, kissed her and said ''remember, we're doing this for our family; you got this'. Monica held her stomach and started helping Dale wipe her face.

Are you good, sis Kiesha asked as they walked back into the living room'. Yeah, girl, the baby decided she didn't like what I ate before I got here; she laughed'. "Wait, it's a girl Jamal said'. Man, she's just talking. We don't even know yet; I feel like I bust nuts that make boys. They all looked at him and bust out laughing; Jamal said nigga that ain't how it works''.

That night, once again, Kiesha looked at her little family and thought to herself, here's another change coming my way; embrace it, girl, you're happy for them. They danced, played games, and ate, '' Just like old times, she thought to herself. Time flew by them as they were enjoying each other's company. Ok babe, Monica said to Dale, mommas can't do these all-nighters anymore, it's time to get me back home and into bed. Yeah, you're right. Let's get my little man home. Jamal looked at Dale and repeated Congratulations. Call me tomorrow so we can talk. They all said good night before they ended their night.

After they left, Kiesha said Mal, here me out. I get what they're saying, but don't they seem real fuckin off to you? Monica is lying to me about something. I feel it. I agree, but baby, we are getting married in a couple of weeks, and I want you to focus on that. Whatever they got going on let them handle it. ''Now come and let daddy take that worried look off your face; leave this shit until the morning. I'm about to make love to you real good tonight.. ''Shit, you should have said that from the beginning Kiesha said, laughing as they ran to their bedroom.

CHAPTER 24

Baby girl, I need to talk to you about something, come to the house at noon. Kiesha woke up reading the text from her father. Dam, I didn't even know he was back. She replied, ok, pops, I'll be there. She laid around the house until it was time to meet her dad. As Kiesha approached the house, she saw a car she thought she recognized, but she shook it off, thinking to herself, what would a corner boy be doing at my parents' house?

What's up pop! Baby girl? Your early David said. Ok, is that a problem Kiesha asked, being taken aback by her father's statement. No, but I did say 12; skipping over her comment, Kiesha asked him about the car she had seen leaving. Pops, who was that leaving when I was pulling up? Baby girl, your business is over at your house, and my business is over here," he said with laughter, but he was serious as hell.

Please sit down; I want to talk to you about something, ok she said as she followed him into the living room. So, I've been looking into Jamal recently. Why are you looking into Jamal? I want to make sure he's the right person, and I'm concerned because there doesn't seem to be much information about him. So, please tell me everything that you know about Jamal. No, the fuck I will not'. What did you say? David asked. Listen, Daddy, we are getting married in two weeks and you are not about to start shit with Jamal before our wedding; now, if you would like to have a sit-down conversation with him man-to-man, you can, but I'm telling you now stop looking into my husband."

Well, he won't be your husband until I make sure this nigga is correct, he seems to perfect baby girl. Do you mean like you? Kiesha said. That shit took David by surprise. Pops, I have always loved how you were with Mom, and that's how Jamal is with me; please don't do this. It's not an option, baby girl. Until I get more information about this nigga you are not marrying him. Pops, you can't make that choice, and I will marry him. Then I won't be there. I'm not going to allow you to marry this nigga, and then we find out some shit about him. Kiesha started crying and stood up and said" I wish you would put your resources into finding out who killed my mother instead of Jamal". For the first time in her life ever, she felt the pain her mother had felt for so many years, and she didn't even know it. David had slapped her across the face.

"Don't you ever talk to me like that again'. Holding her face, she looked at her father, a stranger to her now, and said stay the fuck away from me, my husband, and our wedding as she ran out of the house and headed home to Jamal. As soon as David did it, the remorse that came over him set in, but he wouldn't let anyone disrespect him, not even his daughter.

CHAPTER 25

Jamal was concerned when he saw Kiesha's number show up seeing she had just told him that she was pulling up to her parent's house. 'Babe, what's wrong? Why are you crying? He hit me, baby, he hit me. Who in the fuck hit you, and where are you? asked Jamal. Screaming, she said my pops, Mal, he slapped me; Jamal was getting angrier and angrier. Baby, stop crying, and please be careful driving. I'll be outside when you pull up. I love you.

Yo, I will kill this nigga Jamal said out loud; he didn't care if that was her father or not; he would never let anyone hurt her. As Kiesha was pulling up, he ran to the car. Babe, what happened? do I need to step to your pops? He asked her while holding her as they walked into the house. Sit here, baby, and tell me everything." Babe, my father has been looking into your background, and he couldn't find anything, so he called me today for me to give him some information on you, and he told me we couldn't get married until he knew everything about you.

When I told him no and told him instead of him putting his resources into you, they should go towards finding out who killed my mother; he slapped me'. I don't want him at our wedding, Mal; my pops has never disrespected me like this before''. Jamal was holding his future wife. Don't worry, baby, he will never hurt you again; let me run you some bath water to relax you. ''Yeah, me and this nigga need to have a talk Jamal thought to himself.

Their day ended early as Jamal bathed his future wife and cuddled her and her cries. Tomorrow, me and Pops will talk, he thought to himself as they both laid there in silence. In the middle of the night, Kiesha got up to go and make her a cup of hot tea; her eyes were so puffy. This was a side of her father she never saw coming. She sat in a big, comfy chair in the living room with a blanket, sipping her tea. ''Mommy, why would pops do this to me? He's never shown an ounce of anger towards me. Did pops ever hit you, mommy? She said out loud. Once again, she found herself crying out for her mother. She finished her tea and climbed back into bed with Jamal.

The next day, Jamal suggested to Kiesha that she take the day to herself: Baby, pamper yourself. I set you up with a massage here at the house, and by the time you're done with that, I'll be home, and we can make dinner, or I'll order out for us, and we can finalize any last-minute wedding plans. Thank you, baby, you're so good to me, Mal; soon I'll be Mrs. Black. She kissed her hubby goodbye. There was no need to ask where he was going because she already knew.

Jamal retrieved David's number from Keisha's phone. Hello Mr. Kelly, who is this David asked'. This is Jamal. We need to talk. 'Nigga why are you calling me?'' I need to speak to you in person. Kiesha came home; ''Let me stop you there. Whatever happened between my fuckin daughter and me is my business, and I know you aren't calling yourself checking me; please tell me you're not. I'm calling you because I hear you're looking into me, so you don't need to look any further; I'm here at your doorstep''.

When David pulled up his security camera, he saw Jamal at his front door. Nigga I'm not there but let me make something very clear to you; I'm not one to be fucked with; now, out of respect for my daughter, I'm going to let this slide. Get the fuck off my steps, I said what I said to my daughter, click. Jamal stared at the camera briefly because he knew David was watching him. Jamal was trying to keep his composure; yeah, this nigga is trippin', fuck him.

After Kiesha's massage, she wanted to call Monica to tell her about her father, but she didn't want to stress her or the baby; she drew herself a bubble bath and decided to put on a two-piece silk Cami set. Jamal came in and said Yo ya, pops is tripping; I'm not feeling this nigga babe, Baby, please, I don't want to talk about him. Even though Jamal was still heated, once again, he loved her so much her wish was his every command.

They ate and watched old movies and went over their guest list for the hundredth time. Well, it's minus one guest because I don’t want him there, Mal; this day is about us and only us.

I’ll let the security know to stop anyone at the door that’s not on this list. We're really about to do this, Kiesha. I love you so much; I knew the moment I laid eyes on you that you were going to be mines. She moved the wedding itinerary over and climbed on top of him. Feeling her pussy through the silk pj’s, Jamal positioned himself in a more comfortable position as he lifted her and himself to slide down his pants.

Dam baby, this pussy feels better and better to me every time I’m inside you he said to her; she started with passionate kisses from his head, face, lips, and finally, his neck as she was slowly rotating her pussy on the head of his dick ’’yeah baby stay right there he said, fuck that shit feel good’’. She held herself up to allow herself to ride the tip of his dick until he took control and guided her all the way down his dick; she let out a seductive moan. They made love until their bodies gave out on them; this love-making session was a session to release stress, pain, and hurt. It was what they both needed.

CHAPTER 26

D Kiesha wants us to stay at the house with them the night before the wedding. She didn't go into full detail, but her and Mr. D had some type of falling out, and he's not coming to the wedding. Dale didn't respond to Monica, he never liked talking about his father. Babe are you listening to me she asked, and he just replied with a yeah'. Starting to show, Monica walked over to Dale and said Baby, you've been having nightmares every night recently; I'm worried about you.

I keep seeing the bodies, Monica; I've done so much shit. My demons are starting to haunt me. Baby, you did what you had to do with T and Slick and everything else because, in your own way, you were trying to protect Jamal and yourself.'. He will never see it like that, Monica, but I had to fuck up our operation. Before he met Kiesha. It didn't matter to me that we were out here doing our shit, but when Kiesha came along, I knew that if our father ever found out what Jamal did, he would dead that nigga. By me robbing the stash houses and fucking shit up with the connect and taking out the niggas I did; I was hoping that Mal would see that he needed to cut his losses and get out of this shit with me.

I've done too much, Monica; I can't wait until we're the fuck out of here; I don't ever want to look back. In 4 days, they will be married, and we will be gone for good.

CHAPTER 27

The morning of the wedding, Kiesha and Jamal woke up to chaos; there was so much going on with them getting ready for the wedding; they didn't want the traditional shit, where the groom and the bride couldn't see each other before the wedding. They stayed with the people they loved and looked at as a family. They did what they did best. They loved on each other all fucking night long until they fell asleep in each other's arms.

Girl, you look so pretty, Monica said, looking at her sister in her wedding dress. Kiesha asked the makeup team to leave the room for a minute. Monica sit with me for a minute, "you have been my best friend my sister for so many years. I don't know what I would do without you, but I understand that we are both on different paths right now. Promise me we will always make time for each other no matter what happens in each other's life.

Sis, you know I love you just as much. We have been through everything, and I wish we were taking these paths together; I want you to see your niece or nephew grow up. We will always be here for each other. She held Kiesha's face in her hands. Mrs. Robyn would be so fuckin proud of you, girlie, I love you. Kiesha interrupted her and said oh, can you ask Dale to come in here.

Dale walked in, and she said Hey bro (which, for the first time, threw him off), hey, I would like to ask you something. Of course, my pops was supposed to walk me down the aisle, but that's no longer an option; would you do the honor of giving me a way to Jamal? Before you answer, we've already talked about it, and once you walk me down then you can go and stand with him, please Dale. You have become my family, and I love you; please do this for me.

Dale grabbed Kiesha and started crying and said yes to her. His heart was filled with so much pain. He wished from the moment he met her that things would have been different, but he knew in his heart that would never be an option. This was one way he could do something for her. Ok, bro nigga man up; I'm supposed to be the one crying; should I take this as yes?

"Hell, yeah, I got you,' he said. Now finish up so you can marry my man. He kissed her on the cheek and walked over to Monica. How's my girls? Girls? Kiesha turned around and looked. It's a girl? Yeah, we found out yesterday; I was supposed to be the one to tell you instead of big mouth over here, Monica said, laughing. Jamal, in the next room, was getting dressed, and he overheard the conversation, yeah nigga get the big guns out because it doesn't matter where you're at. If my niece calls Uncle Mal, I'm coming. Everyone finished getting ready and headed to the church.

Driving in the back of the limo, Jamal said Baby, are you ready for this? Kiesha said Baby, nothing else matters; this shit is for life, and she leaned in with a kiss. She wouldn't let it show, but she wished her father was there but as always, she was used to change. The four entered the back of the church as their guests were coming in through the front. Everyone started taking their seats, and Jamal positioned himself at the altar. Their wedding party was small but what mattered the most were just the four friends that started this together.

Dale walked Monica down first; her belly was protruding out there. When it was time for Kiesha to walk down the aisle, there was no traditional music. She chose the song they first danced to. Jodeci's My heart belongs to you. She looked beautiful; her gown was white and flowing right behind her. Her waist was snatched in, which caused her breasts to sit up perfectly. Jamal slightly grinned as he thought about everything he would do to his wife after this. He was so attracted to her. There, the two stood in front of the pastor, both having their own separate set of emotions, Jamal wishing his big brother was there, and Kiesha wishing her parents were there, but nevertheless, this day was about them. They said their vows, and when the pastor gave them his blessings to kiss, they took full advantage.

Everyone, please welcome Mr. & Mrs. Jamal Black. Everyone stood and clapped as the couple walked out of the wedding. Dale and Monica knew they weren't going to the reception just because they couldn't risk David seeing Dale. The plan was to leave with their bags already in the car, do a once-over of the house, and hit the road.

CHAPTER 28

David sat across the street from the church in an unmarked car. He had to see his daughter on her wedding day, but he knew he needed to stay out of sight, not to make a scene. As he watched his daughter, and her new husband walk out of the church everyone was showing them love. There were so many people gathering around her he was trying to get the best view he could, but the crowd was growing larger and larger. Dale and Monica had already made their way to their car; as Kiesha and Jamal were getting in the limo, Kiesha looked across the street at a car she noticed had been sitting there.

The sun was in her eyes as they locked eyes on each other; she looked again. Was that her father? At the same time David was trying to get a better view the unthinkable happened. His son, his wife's killer, drove past him. I know I didn't just see who I thought I had seen. David tried to hurry and make a U-turn but the street was so crowded that he wasn't able to. He started flipping the fuck out. Why is he here? Was he at the wedding? Does he know Jamal? For the first time, panic had set in with him.

Fuck Fuck, Dale said, hitting the steering wheel; Baby, what's wrong? David was there. He saw me, baby; he saw me. We have to go now ain't no time to return to the house. But D, we still have to get more shit; I told you, Monica, to take what we could; this nigga will have everybody out here looking for us. We have to go now!!! We will stop at a hotel somewhere far away to rest, but this is the last time we will see Buffalo. David is going to have every hitta out here looking for me.

Yo, meet me at the spot ASAP, David's text to Knock said. Arriving at the reception Kiesha and Jamal noticed that Dale or Monica hadn't arrived. Baby, I'm calling their phones, and they're not answering she said to her new husband. Jamal took her phone and turned it off ''Baby, today is our day. Whatever anybody else is doing, that's them, but today I'm going to enjoy my new wife, and she's going to enjoy her new husband.'' They walked into the reception hall dancing to (you guessed it) On the run! This song meant more to them than anyone knew.

The reception was lit with music, food, weed, and drinks. They were enjoying the beginning of their new life. I love you Mrs. Black. I'm going to make you so happy. You already do, baby; this shit is for life. Jamal had already given the limo driver specific instructions when he rented the limo that he wanted one that had soundproofed and dark-tinted windows between them and the driver.

Sitting in the back of the limo, sparking a blunt, Jamal sat between his wife's legs as she smoked on her blunt. He took her panties off and ate her pussy as she came over and over. Her hand wrapped in his freshly twisted dreads; she was fucking the fuck out of his face. He turned her around in the limo and spread her legs open and took the pleasure of making love and fucking his wife at the same time.

Once they arrived at their home, they said thank you to the driver, and they went into the house to continue their session. We're not sleeping tonight, baby. I have a new appreciation for your body, and I'm about to do things to you that you could never imagine. Jamal kept his word; every room in that house saw a new version of them that night. Morning comes, and Kiesha says good morning, husband; I can barely walk with laughter. Shit, that was the plan he replied.

They enjoyed breakfast together, and then Kiesha said, can we talk about Monica and Dale? Yes, my wife, call Monica and I'll call him. Let's see what's up with these two No answer after several attempts. Babe, before we leave tonight, can we go and check on them, please? I want to make sure her and the baby are ok. Yeah, our plane leaves at 6:45, so we can head out there and then go to the airport. The two spent the rest of the day packing and preparing for their honeymoon. The two were in their own world,they never knew they were being watched as they drove to Dale's house in Dunkirk.

Once they got there, they noticed neither car was there, and they both were blowing up Dale and Monica's phone, ok now I'm worried Jamal said as they went around to the back of Dale's house; Jamal knew how to get into his house in case of emergencies. Once they were in and started looking around, it was clear that they had left town and in a hurry.

Jamal took out his phone again, yo D call me now; what the fuck is going on, nigga? I'm at your crib; what's up? They didn't know Dale and Monica had already gotten rid of their old phones. Kiesha walks through the house looking through their cabinets and closets. Dam Monica, where are you sis? She gets to their bedroom, and she sits on the bed, trying to figure shit out. She looks down, and she sees a book sticking out from under the bed.

As she picks the book up, she realizes Monica was making a diary and she opens it and starts reading it. Jamal yells from the front room; baby will have to leave; I'm going to the car to get my other phone to call this nigga, and then we out.

''I love her so much, but how do I tell her he killed her mother; how do I tell her he's, her brother? I wish I would have never found those pictures of Mrs. Robyn dead. I can't look her in her face; Mr. D is Scar like wtf. This is going to kill Kiesha 'But I can't let her take Dale from me. He's the father of my child, and I love him.''

Kiesha stood on the bed, frozen as she looked at the book; when she went to close the book, pictures of her, David, and Robyn's lifeless body fell out. She lost it, she started screaming, she ran with the book to the front door calling for Jamal as he was sitting in the car still trying to call Dale and anyone else that might know where he was. She reached the front door, and Jamal could hear her screaming; he got ready to get out the car. Baby, what's wrong, what's wrong? he said. Then Kiesha looks at a familiar vehicle, slowly pulling up towards Jamal, and she realizes it's the car that was at her father's house. With no warning, Jamal was so focused on getting to Kiesha, he never saw it coming. Knock was in the driver's seat, and he pulled up to Jamal and, let two off into his chest and speed off.

Jamal fell to the ground as Kiesha screamed and called out for help,'' Baby, please no, omg somebody fucking help me as she cried as Jamal lay dying in her arms. Don't leave me; please don't leave me, please help me, somebody, as people gathered around her. When the police arrived, Kiesha was unconsolable; she wasn't making any sense as they took her to the hospital, and she watched the coroner take her husband away. While sitting in the room at the hospital waiting for the detectives, she remembered she had Monica's book. She took it out and started rereading it.

She read about everything Dale had confided in Monica; about the beatings her mother endured by her father, Dale killing her mother, Monica keeping it a secret, and David being the drug lord Scar that she had always heard about. They all betrayed me, she said as she looked at Jamal's blood on her hands, they all fucking betrayed me. I will kill every last one of them, including that bastard baby inside of her. I will kill him for taking my mother away from me, and I'm going to save the last bullet for the mutha fucka who started all of this, David Kelly. She got up and looked out the door to make sure the ghost was clear as she went to the morgue to see Jamal's body; they won't see me coming; I promise you that baby, I will make them all pay. I love you, baby. My family and my friends betrayed me; the streets are what I gave my life to, and the Streets Betrayed Me.

THE END…..

Coming Soon.

The Streets Betrayed Me 2

Made in the USA
Middletown, DE
31 October 2024